THE BATTERED BADGE

THE BATTERED BADGE

A Nero Wolfe Mystery

Robert Goldsborough

MYSTERIOUSPRESS.COM

OPEN ROAD

INTEGRATED MEDIA

NEW YORK

Cover design by Ian Koviak

Author photo by Colleen Berg

978-1-5040-4910-8

Published in 2018 by MysteriousPress.com/Open Road Integrated Media, Inc.
180 Maiden Lane
New York, NY 10038
www.mysteriouspress.com
www.openroadmedia.com

To Jane Stroh and all the fine women

who have served so ably over the years at The Book Store

in Glen Ellyn, Illinois

THE BATTERED BADGE

CHAPTER 1

As is my custom each morning, I settle in at the small table in the kitchen reading the *New York Times* and devouring one of Fritz Brenner's superb breakfasts. On the menu this gray November day were fresh-squeezed orange juice, brioches, grilled ham, and grape-thyme jelly. Up in his bedroom, Nero Wolfe was feasting on the same items while also, presumably, reading his own copy of the *Times*.

Most mornings, I find little to interest me in the newspaper that claims, in a small box tucked into the upper left-hand corner of page one, that it delivers "All the News That's Fit to Print." Today, however, I did see a story that got my attention, in large part because it involved someone both Wolfe and I know, and know well.

The headline: "Local Reformer Pierce Gunned Down on Park Avenue." The story reported that Lester Pierce, fifty-six, the executive director of the Good Government Group, known popularly as either Three-G or GGG, had been killed by pistol shots from a passing car as he climbed out of a taxi and crossed the sidewalk toward the front entrance of the luxury co-op building where he and his wife lived in a duplex apartment.

It was the story's next few paragraphs that stopped me:

Mr. Pierce had built his reputation as a reformer primarily on his attacks upon the New York Police Department for what he claimed is its laxity involving the crime syndicate. His vitriol was particularly intense when directed at Inspector Lionel T. Cramer, longtime head of the department's Homicide Squad.

"Cramer must be removed from his post, sooner rather than later, and I will not rest until that blessed event occurs," Mr. Pierce had said at a press conference earlier this month. The police department did not react to Mr. Pierce's statement then, and at press time, the department has issued no comment about his death. The *Times* was unable to reach Mr. Cramer for a comment.

"We in the Good Government Group will not rest until the perpetrator of this brazen crime is brought to justice," said Roland Marchbank, the assistant executive director of the group. "We call upon the New York City Police Department to use every resource at its disposal to expose the murderer."

When Wolfe came down at eleven from his morning session with the orchids in the plant rooms, I held up my copy of the *Times* as he settled in at his desk and rang for beer.

"I saw it," he said.

"What do you think?"

"Mr. Cramer has been besieged in the past, and doubtless will be in the future as well. Such is the nature of his station."

"You don't feel this is a little more serious than some of the inspector's past scrapes?"

Wolfe raised his shoulders a quarter inch, then let them drop. For him, that constitutes a shrug.

"I don't know, but it seems to me that with the murder of this Pierce character, the heat will be unlike anything Cramer has ever been exposed to before," I persisted. Wolfe's response was to go through the morning mail I had opened and placed on his desk blotter. The discussion was closed.

Three days passed, and the Pierce murder stayed on the front page of all the papers, each of them trying—without success—to find new angles. The *Daily News* and the *Post* each ran editorials demanding that the police department give daily progress reports. The *Post* questioned whether Cramer had been in his job too long: "Perhaps it is time for a change at the top of the Homicide Squad."

I was in the office typing up correspondence that morning when Wolfe came down from the plant rooms. He had barely gotten himself settled at his desk when the telephone squawked. I answered, as I always do during business hours, "Nero Wolfe's office, Archie Goodwin speaking."

"It's me, Archie," the caller rasped. I was momentarily speechless, as that voice on the other end belonged to none other than Sergeant Purley Stebbins, Inspector Cramer's longtime right-hand man and one who almost never calls me "Archie." To him, I am "Goodwin" if he even bothers to utter my name at all.

Even rarer is Stebbins calling us at the brownstone. He has never much liked Wolfe or me, and the feeling is mutual. In the world as Purley sees it, there is no room whatever for private detectives, even though he invariably accompanies Cramer to West Thirty-Fifth Street for what the inspector refers to as Wolfe's "charades," those times when all the suspects of a crime are gathered in the office and Wolfe invariably fingers the guilty party for Cramer—and for himself, since he ends up getting his fee from a client for solving the crime.

"What can I do for you, Purley?" I asked, trying to keep the irritation out of my voice.

I could hear deep breathing. "I would like to come and see Mr. Wolfe," he said slowly, as if having rehearsed the line.

"May I ask why?" I knew he was struggling, and darned if I was going to make things any easier for him. If that sounds mean-spirited, then I haven't been clear about just how deep the rancor between us runs.

"It's about the inspector," he said in a voice just above a whisper. "I'd . . . rather not talk about it on the telephone."

I cupped my mouthpiece and turned to Wolfe, who was perusing an orchid catalog that had arrived in the morning mail. "It is Sergeant Stebbins," I said. "He wants to come and talk to you about Cramer. He doesn't want to say anything more on the phone."

Wolfe made a face. "Confound it, why can't the man just tell us what he—oh, very well, tell him to be here at three."

I passed that word along to Purley, who muttered that he would be coming. There was no "thank you" from him, but then, that would be out of character.

"So the sergeant himself will be coming to see you, hat in hand, so to speak," I said after hanging up. "What do you think of that?"

"He obviously is concerned about his superior, although I do not know that I can be of any assistance. However, I have agreed to see the sergeant, and I shall," Wolfe said, opening his current book, *Profiles in Courage* by John F. Kennedy. If he had any concern about our afternoon visitor, he did not show it.

I put Stebbins out of my mind during lunch, which was veal cutlets and Fritz's special mixed salad of endive, romaine, Bibb lettuce, celery, carrot curls, and grated, cooked beets with devil's rain dressing, followed by pumpkin pie à la mode.

We were back in the office with coffee five minutes before three when the doorbell rang. I went down the hall to the front door and through the one-way glass saw the bony, square-jawed face of Sergeant Purley Stebbins.

Pulling open the door, I nodded and got a nod in return. Purley and I never have been big on conversation. "You know the way," I said after I had taken his coat and hung it on the hall rack. I expected our guest to take the red leather chair at the end of Wolfe's desk, but he fooled me and chose one of the yellow ones. Maybe he figured the only cop entitled to sit in the place of honor was his longtime boss.

"Mr. Stebbins, would you care for something to drink?" Wolfe asked. "As you see, I am having beer."

"Nothing for me, thanks," Purley said. His oversize ears were red, and he obviously was uneasy, given his past experiences with Wolfe.

"Does Mr. Cramer know you are here?"

"He does not, and I would like to keep it that way."

Wolfe nodded. "You requested this meeting, sir. What is your agenda?"

"The inspector has been ordered to take administrative leave, and I am pretty sure that they are out to get him off the force and maybe even charged," the sergeant replied.

"Who are 'they'?"

Purley shifted in the chair and frowned. "It's really Commissioner O'Hara, although he's getting a push from that so-called good government bunch. They haven't come right out and said so, but they believe the inspector had something to do with Lester Pierce's death, and they've got O'Hara believing it, too, which isn't hard to do."

"Twaddle! Mr. Cramer is even less likely than I to commit murder, or to plan one."

"Yes, sir. Commissioner O'Hara has never liked the inspector."

"What are his reasons?"

"I know that you and I haven't always been on the of best terms, Mr. Wolfe, but I feel that I can trust you. I would not want what I say here to be repeated."

"Things discussed in this office are assumed to be confidential, unless of course they have a direct bearing upon criminal activity. You may speak candidly. Mr. Goodwin is every bit as closemouthed as am I."

Purley's expression remained impassive, which is usually the case. He leaned forward, elbows on knees. "As you both know, O'Hara took over the commissioner's office when Skinner retired. He always resented Skinner and felt that he should have gotten the job a lot sooner. Since O'Hara's been in office he has tried to get rid of all the old guard, and he has been damned successful. The inspector is the only department head left from the Skinner era, and I believe the commissioner is looking for an excuse to get rid of him as well."

"Who is the acting head of Homicide in Mr. Cramer's enforced absence?" Wolfe asked.

"Captain Rowcliff," Purley said, unable to keep the contempt out of his voice. George Rowcliff, who was promoted from lieutenant a year ago, ranks as the least-favorite cop of both Wolfe and me. On the plus side, he has been awarded medals for bravery over the years and is moderately handsome, if you overlook his pop eyes and his snarly voice. On the negative side, he once arrived at the brownstone with some underlings and a warrant. Under Rowcliff's direction they conducted a search, which earned him Wolfe's lasting enmity, as well as an apology to Wolfe, ordered by then boss-man Skinner.

When Rowcliff gets irritated or flustered, he starts to stutter and can't stop himself. On several occasions, I have seen him on the verge of this situation and began stuttering myself, which really got Rowcliff going. I probably should be ashamed but I am not, which tells you volumes about my attitude toward the man.

"Well, he has always wanted to run Homicide," I told Purley, "and now he's got the opportunity. Do you think he'll get the post permanently if Cramer ends up out of a job?"

"Yeah, it's possible. And if the inspector goes, then of course I'm gone, too," the sergeant said, pounding a meaty fist on his knee. "It's bad enough now, with Rowcliff ordering me around like some sort of errand boy. He resents me because he sees me as 'Cramer's guy.'"

"I sympathize with your frustration," Wolfe said, "but I fail to see how I can be of any help."

"Maybe you can't, but I know that you respect the inspector, even though the two of you haven't always seen eye-to-eye. I just wanted you to know the situation. I don't have the money to afford your rates, but if the inspector is indirectly charged with the murder of Lester Pierce, as I think will happen, he's going to need someone on his side."

Wolfe raised his eyebrows. "I believe such a charge to be highly unlikely."

"Possibly," Purley said, "but I can tell you this much: at the moment, the inspector has no one in his corner, not the press, not that so-called Good Government Group, not the current police commissioner, and certainly not Captain Rowcliff, who would like nothing more than to stab his former boss in the back and take over his chair for good. Well, I have said my piece and I will be going." He looked at me and said, "Don't bother to see me out; I know the way."

The sergeant rose slowly and lumbered down the hall to the front door, with me following just to make sure he left, and I closed the door behind him. Old habits die hard.

"Well, just what do you make of all that?" I asked Wolfe when I got back to the office and eased into my desk chair.

"Mr. Stebbins is clearly troubled or he would not have come to us today. I hardly need tell you we are not among his favorite people. This visit cannot have been easy for the sergeant."

"Well, he certainly is no favorite of yours. Of course, neither is Cramer, for that matter."

"Archie, I neither like nor dislike Mr. Stebbins. The same is true of my attitude toward Inspector Cramer. That, however, is not the case where Mr. Rowcliff is concerned."

"Yeah, I will add an amen to that. That man is in a class by himself, or a lack of class. So, now what?"

"I do not see myself as being an advocate for Mr. Cramer. He is capable of taking care of himself, as he has manifestly shown over the years. Do you agree?"

"He's tough, no question. And the two of you have butted heads more times than I can begin to count. But do we want to trade Cramer in and take our chances with Rowcliff every time we have to deal with the New York police?"

Wolfe leaned back and closed his eyes. "It is out of our hands," he said, blinking, getting to his feet, and heading for the elevator. It was time for his afternoon visit with the ten thousand orchids in the plant rooms on the roof.

CHAPTER 2

For the next hour, I typed up the correspondence to orchid growers that Wolfe had dictated the day before and put Inspector Cramer's plight out of my mind. However, a phone call changed that. It was Lon Cohen of the *New York Gazette*.

"Haven't heard from you lately, other than at our Thursday night poker games," I told him. "I seem to recall that I took more than a few dollars from you last week in the largest pot of the evening."

"It was bound to happen sometime," Lon said. "Even the mighty Yankees occasionally have themselves an off day."

"Even when you lose, you act like you've won," I grumbled. "To what do we owe this intrusion?"

"Intrusion, you say? That's a fine way to treat an old friend. I thought I would just check in and see what you folks are up to."

If you are new to these stories, you need to know that Lon Cohen is a longtime *Gazette* writer and editor. He currently does not have a title I am aware of, but he occupies an office high up in the newspaper's Midtown building, just three doors down the hall from the publisher. He has gotten some dandy scoops from us over the years, but he also has supplied us with valuable information on individuals and events that were vital to cases Wolfe and I have worked on.

"You never 'just check in' on us," I told him. "Come on now, out with it. Don't be coy."

"As usual, you have seen right through me," Lon said with a theatrical sigh. "I simply have got to stop being so transparent. Okay, I'll come clean: I am wondering if you have heard from your old buddy Inspector Cramer lately."

"He is hardly what I would term our old buddy, as you well know, but back to your question. Is there any reason why we should have heard from him?"

"I know you read the papers, including this morning's *Times*. The inspector finds himself in a whole lot of trouble, possibly more than at any time in his long career."

"So it would seem. But where do we come in?"

"Well, this may sound crazy, but I'm curious as to whether Cramer has gone to Wolfe for help."

"Lon, that doesn't just *sound* crazy, it *is* crazy. The man would sooner jump off the George Washington Bridge than turn to Nero Wolfe for help."

"Okay, okay, so maybe I was reaching."

"I'll say you were. But since you are on the wire and it's your dime, what do the boys on the *Gazette* who cover the police beat think about Cramer's situation?"

"They believe that he's finished as the head of Homicide, and based on what they have been hearing, he may also end up getting indicted."

"What for?"

"Close ties and dealings with, shall we say . . . certain undesirables."

"Meaning?"

"Meaning, of course, members of the crime syndicate, Archie."

"Oh, come on now! This is Inspector Cramer we're talking about, not some sleazy copper like that lieutenant who got sent up last year for filling his pockets with soiled money."

"I must remind you that the man you refer to as a 'sleazy copper' once was among the most honored and decorated members of the department. It is amazing how the lure of great amounts of money can alter an individual's behavior."

"Are you suggesting Cramer is on the take?"

"I am suggesting such a possibility," Lon said, "as far-fetched as that may sound to you."

"Sorry, my headline-hunting friend, but I am not buying what you seem to be selling. I am by no means a close friend of the inspector, but I do feel I know the man fairly well, given all the times Wolfe and I have had run-ins and other dealings with him over the years, and I cannot conceive of his consorting with the mob."

"Suit yourself," Lon said. "But be prepared for the possibility that Cramer's reputation may end up being tarnished, or worse—and I mean a lot worse."

"You are just filled with good cheer today, aren't you? But then, what should I expect from a member of—what do you call it?—the Fourth Estate. None of you are ever happy unless you've got some grim news to trot out for your avid and hungry reading public."

"You have cut me to the quick, my longtime poker patsy. And here I was just trying to alert you to a problem involving a man you and Nero Wolfe have known for years, however you choose to define your relationship with him."

"I would look upon your call as an act of altruism if I were not by nature the suspicious type."

"Meaning?"

"Meaning that I believe you to be on a fishing expedition to learn whether one Lionel T. Cramer has been seeking our assistance. I can only repeat my earlier comment about the inspector and the George Washington Bridge. Since we are on the subject, just what leads you and your police reporters to believe Cramer is consorting with those on the wrong side of the law?"

"Aha, so I have whetted your curiosity, have I?"

"Let us stipulate that I have a healthy curiosity."

"Is that what you call it? All right, Archie, certain of our . . . shall we say informants . . . have said soon after Pierce's killing, the inspector was seen dining in the back room of a certain Italian restaurant on Mulberry Street down in Little Italy."

"Since when is dining on spaghetti and meatballs an indication of suspicious behavior?"

"It's not the dining per se, but just whom he was dining with and the venue."

"Okay, I will bite, pardon the pun."

"Sorry, I won't pardon it, I've got my standards," Lon replied. "But since you asked, Cramer's dinner partner was one Ralph Mars, and that particular restaurant's back room is a favorite meeting place of people who prefer privacy."

"But somehow, I gather the *Gazette* has found ways to circumvent that privacy."

"It is well known that restaurant kitchen staffs are underpaid. I will say no more."

"Heaven forbid. This is, of course, *the* Ralph Mars, longtime underworld kingpin."

"Well, to be specific, he wasn't born with that surname. But, yes, you have correctly identified him."

"The great Tony Bennett wasn't born Tony Bennett either, but that doesn't seem to bother anyone. Everyone, Italians included, has every right to change their name. Did your restaurant kitchen spies happen to eavesdrop and learn the content of the conversation between Messrs. Cramer and Mars?"

"Unfortunately, they did not," Lon said.

"So, for all you know, the two may have been discussing the Giants' last-second victory over the Pittsburgh Steelers last Sunday. Everybody else has been talking about it."

"Somehow, I don't think football was the subject of their talk, Archie."

"All right, what *do* you think?"

"I'm not sure, but doesn't it seem odd that one of the city's top cops is seen breaking bread with a top hoodlum in a room known for clandestine meetings?"

"I concede that to be an unusual occurrence. But I have seen no mention whatever of the backroom meeting in your dear old *Gazette*, and I pride myself on going through the paper thoroughly every day."

"We . . . don't have enough to go on," Lon conceded.

"Is that so now? You said earlier that, if I may paraphrase, 'based on what the *Gazette*'s police reporters have been hearing, Cramer may get indicted.' Care to elaborate on that?"

"Not at present. But you have got to admit, Archie, that on top of the heat Cramer had already been getting from the Three-G group, followed by Pierce's murder, things don't look so good for him to be supping with the shadowy Mr. Mars."

"All right, I will concede that to be unusual behavior on the inspector's part, to say the least. But this is still circumstantial evidence of malfeasance, or whatever you want to call it."

"I know that your boss also reads both our paper and the *Times* thoroughly every day. Does he have any opinion as to Cramer's job security?"

"Mr. Wolfe says in effect that the inspector has been in plenty of pickles before and he likely will be in others in the future. He does not seem overly concerned."

"Well, tell him that he should be prepared for a great fall," Lon said.

"I will, and I'll tell you his reaction when next we meet, which will be at Saul Panzer's poker table on Thursday."

"I can hardly wait to get even for last week, Archie," Lon said as we both hung up.

CHAPTER 3

When Wolfe came down from the plant rooms at six and settled with a beer in his reinforced chair, I recounted my conversation with Lon Cohen, including the episode in the back room of that notorious Italian eatery. He leaned back, saying nothing. I was about to make a comment when the phone jangled and I answered in the usual way.

"Mr. Goodwin, this is David Watkins of the *Times*. I would like to speak to Nero Wolfe."

"May I tell him the nature of this call, Mr. Watkins?"

"I want to get his thoughts on the predicament Inspector Lionel T. Cramer of the Homicide Squad finds himself in. I know that in the past, Mr. Wolfe has been helpful to the inspector in his investigations."

"Just a moment," I said, cupping the mouthpiece and turning to Wolfe. "It's David Watkins of the *Times*. He wants to ask you about Cramer's situation."

"I have nothing to say!"

"How would you like me to phrase that to the man?"

Wolfe frowned and picked up his receiver while I stayed on the line.

"This is Nero Wolfe," he barked.

"Yes, Mr. Wolfe. David Watkins of the *Times*. We are interested in getting your thoughts on Inspector Cramer being placed on administrative leave. Do you believe such to be fair treatment of a man who has served this city for so long?"

"Mr. Watkins, I am not in possession of sufficient information to venture an opinion on this matter."

"But surely you have some thoughts," Watkins persisted.

"I am not about to speculate on Mr. Cramer's situation without adequate knowledge of the specifics. Good day, sir," Wolfe said as he cradled his instrument.

Watkins began a new sentence, although all I heard was "But . . ." before the connection got severed.

"Now are you satisfied?" Wolfe said, glaring at me and returning to his book and his beer.

"Look, you are a public figure, whether you happen to like that or not," I told him. "People like reading about you. Besides, I know you enjoy seeing your name in print—don't try to deny it." That earned me another glare, so I removed myself and went to the kitchen to see how Fritz was progressing with dinner—squabs with sauce Vénitienne.

The squabs were superb as usual, as were the cherry tarts that followed. Wolfe has a hard-and-fast policy to not discuss cases at mealtime, but because we did not presently have a case, he chose—much to my surprise—to expound on our long and often stormy relationship with Inspector Cramer.

"I realize Mr. Cramer and his current situation are on your mind, Archie," he said. "I concur with your judgment that we would far prefer working with the inspector than with that . . . *man*, Rowcliff." Wolfe pronounced "man" as if it were a disease.

"But to borrow a phrase I have heard you use in regard to your weekly poker game," he continued, "we must play the hand we are dealt. And in this instance, our hand leaves us little choice but to stay out of the game, whatever our wishes. You know as well as I do that Mr. Cramer would not solicit our help, even if we had aid to give—which at present we do not. Are you in agreement?"

"I am. I simply cannot believe he is involved either in Pierce's shooting or with the crime syndicate. But as you say, the inspector would never approach us for help. His pride simply will not allow it."

"He is an obstinate individual, as we have observed over time: competent, generally; mercurial, occasionally; brave and honest, unquestionably," Wolfe said. "But he also is maddeningly stubborn and intractable, as we have experienced. Do you have anything to add to that appraisal?"

"No, sir, you have nailed it," I said to my boss, who also can be maddeningly stubborn and intractable, although I agreed with his position in this instance. "I see no choice for us but to sit this one out."

CHAPTER 4

The next morning's *Times* had a short article about Cramer on page twelve, reporting in essence that he remained on administrative leave and that Commissioner O'Hara had declined to make a statement. Wolfe's name did appear in the piece, which may or may not have pleased him as he reviewed a copy of the paper in his bedroom with breakfast. It read: "Nero Wolfe, the well-known private investigator who has collaborated with Mr. Cramer on numerous murder cases, had no comment regarding the inspector's current situation."

The phone rang as I sat in the office with a postbreakfast coffee. It was Lon Cohen. "Is this now to be a daily ritual?" I asked.

"No sarcasm, Archie; it does not become you. I feel I have a solemn responsibility to keep you and your boss apprised on developments in *l'affaire Cramer.*"

"Getting pretty hoity-toity with the French now, aren't we? Okay, what gives?"

"It seems that one of the people calling for the inspector's scalp has an ax to grind, so to speak."

"And yet you refuse to pardon me when I try to get cute with words. Very punny."

"Okay, okay, let's call a truce."

"Fine by me. Now who is this with the ax to grind?"

"Weldon Dunagan; I'm sure you've heard of him."

"The grocery store tycoon, right? These days there are DunaganMarts from coast to coast."

"And now some overseas as well," Lon said. "The chain has grown like crazy in recent years, mainly by advertising and marketing what they claim are wholesome and unprocessed natural foods."

"So what is Dunagan's gripe with Cramer?"

"One of our reporters with a good memory recalled that years ago, Cramer helped to break up a beating on the street."

"Oh yeah, I remember it now. The inspector was being driven home to Queens from his office one night, and he and his chauffeur, a patrolman, saw two young punks pounding on a third guy on a street in Long Island City. It got some news coverage at the time."

"I remember it, too," Lon said. "But what I had forgotten, if I ever even knew it, was that one of the jerks doing the beating was Dunagan's son, Kevin. Of course, it may not have registered with me at the time because the elder Dunagan was not nearly as well known as he is today."

"And so he's still holding a grudge against Cramer, is that it?"

"Yeah, especially since the inspector was a witness at Kevin's trial, and the kid ended up getting some prison time."

"That had to make Daddy angry."

"There's more, Archie. Weldon Dunagan is far and away the largest financial supporter of the Good Government Group.

And there's still more: Dunagan has been heard to say, 'I'll see that so-and-so Cramer get tossed off the force if it's the last thing that I ever do.' Except that the man did not say 'so-and-so,' if you happen to get my drift."

"I do. And I assume Dunagan has a lot of influence, including with people in local government."

"You assume correctly."

"Why hasn't Dunagan's comment about Cramer ever been in print? Or did I miss it?"

"The same reason Cramer's dinner in Little Italy with Ralph Mars hasn't been reported," Lon said. "We simply don't have enough to go on, only hearsay, and my guess is the other papers don't either, assuming that they even know as much as we do."

"Well, I have to believe that sooner or later, all this stuff involving Cramer will come out."

"I have to agree," Lon said, "and things will only get worse for the inspector, although he is not the only one feeling the heat from Dunagan on the Pierce murder. We hear that the grocery king feels the whole police department is falling down on the job regarding the investigation. He apparently has had some angry conversations with Commissioner O'Hara. We can't confirm this, but I think our source in the police department is pretty solid, even though he insists on remaining anonymous."

Just as we hung up, Wolfe entered the office with a raceme of yellow *Cymbidium*, placed it in the vase on his desk, and rang for beer. He was barely settled in his chair when the phone rang. I answered in the usual way and got rewarded with the rasping voice of Inspector Cramer. "Wolfe there? What am I saying—of course he is—it's after eleven!"

I mouthed our caller's name, and my boss frowned, picking up his receiver while I stayed on the line. "This is Nero Wolfe."

"Listen, Wolfe, the last thing I need right now is to see your name in any story that has anything to do with me. Do you understand that?"

"If you please, Mr. Cramer!" Wolfe snapped. "I did not initiate a conversation with that reporter on the *Times*, and as you have read, I made no comment whatever about your situation— nor do I plan to."

After several seconds of silence, Cramer exhaled, saying, "All right . . . all right," in a tired tone. He hung up.

I turned to Wolfe, who popped the cap on the first of two bottles of chilled Remmers on the tray Fritz had brought in. "All I can say is if that's a sample of what life is like in the Cramer household these days, I feel sorry for the inspector's wife, having to put up with a caged lion."

"These are not felicitous times for Mr. Cramer, Archie, as we already have discussed. The man finds himself under siege. He is hardly to be envied."

"Well, I, for one, feel sorry for the guy. I never thought I would be saying that, given the times he's hauled me in for questioning or threatened to toss me into the Tombs and throw away the key."

"To a degree I share your reaction," Wolfe said. "Inspector Cramer over the years has incurred our animosity on numerous occasions, but if he is forced from his job permanently, the police department and the city will be the poorer for it."

"But, as you have stated before and I concur, there is not a hell of a lot we can do," I said. That ended our discussion concerning the inspector's plight, at least for the present.

CHAPTER 5

For the next week, I thought about Inspector Cramer no more than two or three times, and then only in passing. I had plenty to keep me occupied, between typing up Wolfe's twenty-page essay on the many hybrids of *Phalaenopsis* for an orchid publication and helping Lily Rowan with the benefit she was hosting for the Humane Society.

A few words here about Lily: she and I have been friends, make that *very good* friends, ever since that day years ago in a pasture in Upstate New York when an angry bull charged me and I avoided its horns only by leaping awkwardly over a fence.

"Very good, Escamillo!" she said, clapping as she observed my jump from her vantage point on the safe side of said fence. For those of you unfamiliar with opera, as I was before I met Lily, Escamillo is a bullfighter in *Carmen*.

Lily is very beautiful and also very rich, having inherited millions from her Irish-born father, who made his fortune building much of Manhattan's sewer system. She also is very lazy, by her own admission. I disagree with this self-description, however, as she consistently uses her wealth for numerous good causes. She has a penthouse slightly smaller than New Hampshire on the roof of a ten-story building on East Sixty-Third Street between Madison and Park Avenues, and she thinks nothing of throwing her home open for charitable events of all sorts. She also thinks nothing of enlisting my help at these soirees, and I have been known to do everything from hanging up visitors' coats to tending the bar in her ballroom-size salon while a string quartet played Mozart and Beethoven.

For the record, as big as Lily's bank balance is, whenever we go out, whether to dinner, dancing, the theater, or a Rangers' game at the Garden, I pay—period. Call it old-fashioned if you insist, but that's the way it is and the way it will always be.

As we dined at Rusterman's Restaurant one evening, she leaned forward out of the blue and asked, "What do you and Mr. Wolfe think about . . . Uncle . . . about Mr. Cramer's predicament?"

Another thing about Lily: Her late father had been a good friend of Cramer's and through his Tammany Hall connections had helped get him on the force years ago. As the inspector told Wolfe and me once, "Lily Rowan's father was one of my best friends. He got me out of a couple of tight holes in the old days when he was on the inside at the Hall. I knew Lily before she could walk."[1]

In fact, Lily once said to me that Cramer had been like an uncle to her, so her anxiety over his situation did not surprise me.

"We are concerned, of course," I told her as we finished our desserts. "For all the wrangling we have done with the inspector

---

1   *Not Quite Dead Enough* by Rex Stout

over the years, both Mr. Wolfe and I know what a good, honest, and generally effective cop he is."

"And of course, you both would much rather deal with him than with that preening jackass Rowcliff," Lily responded, arching an eyebrow.

"Okay, okay," I said, laughing, "so you have a point there. I won't argue it or your description of Rowcliff. On a more practical level, I don't see how we can be of much help to Cramer at present. For one thing, he doesn't want our aid and has told us as much, in no uncertain terms. This even though we haven't even offered to help him. Also, someone has come to us asking that we intercede on the inspector's behalf."

"Sergeant Stebbins, no doubt," Lily said, again arching a well-tended brow.

"Do you have people stationed across the street from the brownstone?" I asked as we both laughed. "Seriously, maybe you can be of some help here, assuming we ever do get involved."

"*Moi?*" Lily said. Now both eyebrows went up.

"Yes, you, my love. What with all your good works, you are well connected around town, particularly with, shall we say, the power elite?"

"Ah, the power elite, is it, Escamillo? I've never thought of people I know in that term."

"I have to admit I lifted that phrase from a book Mr. Wolfe was reading a while back. I also admit that I've never read the book myself, but I was taken with its title. And you have to concede that you know a lot of people who do wield a substantial amount of power."

Lily rolled her eyes. "Power? Well, I suppose so. But then, powerful people are very often rich people, and I happen to seek out rich people because they have money to give away to good causes. That is, if I can get them to part with some of it."

"Somehow, I don't think you have much trouble in that area."
She shrugged. "I win some, I lose some, but on the whole, I think I have a pretty good batting average, to use a term you're familiar with. Now let us get specific: Whom do you think I can help you with?"

"Because Lester Pierce's shooting is apparently what really got Cramer in the soup, what did you think of Mr. Pierce?"

"You mean Saint Lester? I do not mean to make fun of the dead, but that is what he was called—behind his back, of course—by both friends and foes. He got the 'saint' label for two reasons: One, he was an elder at that big Presbyterian church in Midtown, a title that he wore like a badge; and two, the man acted holier than thou much of the time in his dealings in the community. Pompous would be a good word to describe him."

"You mentioned friends and foes. Who were his foes?"

"The crime syndicate, of course, which did not enjoy his steady stream of attacks on them, which really spoke well for Lester. But a lot of the state's politicians—in both parties—thought all of his self-righteous posturings were a precursor to his running for office. It was widely rumored that he hoped to be governor someday in the not-too-distant future. To him, I think being the head of Three-G wasn't an end in itself, just a stepping-stone to Albany."

"How did you feel about him personally?"

"I met him three or maybe four times at benefit luncheons and such, and I found him to be . . . well, full of a phony sort of bonhomie, like so many politicians and would-be politicians."

"Bonhomie, eh? I'll have to look that one up. I can't remember Wolfe ever even using it."

"See how much you can learn by knowing me?" Lily said. "Consider yourself fortunate."

"Oh, I do, and I have for years. So I gather it is fair to say you were not overly impressed with Mr. Pierce."

"It wasn't just his false friendliness that turned me off. He was tall and handsome, no question, and he was aware of his looks. But he had a reputation—apparently well deserved—as a lothario. You know what that word means, don't you?"

"I do indeed."

"It seems that Saint Lester had himself quite a fling with one of his colleagues at Three-G, one Laura Cordwell, a former beauty queen, Miss Missouri no less, with brains to boot, as in an MBA from Columbia. Their shenanigans were among the least-well-kept secrets in town."

"You are full of juicy tidbits today. You and Lon Cohen should get together and swap stories about the great and the near great in our fair metropolis. I seem to recall that Mr. Pierce had a wife. Did she know about this dalliance?"

"Dalliance? Now you are the one throwing fancy words around, Escamillo. Ever the competitor. The answer is yes, the formidable Audra Kingston Pierce was said to be well aware of her husband's moral . . . deficiencies. For whatever reasons, she apparently chose to ignore them."

"Tell me more about the Widow Pierce."

"I've run into her on a number of occasions, mostly benefit luncheons and cocktail parties. Audra comes from money—lots of it," Lily said. "Old New England wealth. Her family made its fortune in textile mills before that industry deserted Massachusetts and moved to the South. She's an attractive sort of woman, in a glacial sort of way. You get the feeling she acts superior because she really *is* superior. I would hardly call her warm, but she is extremely generous with her money and has given hundreds of thousands to good causes. And she has given her time to these causes as well."

"Did Pierce marry the lady for her dough?" I asked.

"Not at all. He inherited plenty of his own. His father and grandfather were Pittsburgh steel barons. So in a sense, the marriage was a dynastic union."

"Children?"

"Three, all of them grown, of course. They all seem to stay out of the gossip columns. I can't tell you anything about them, I'm afraid, other than I recall at least two, a son and daughter, had big society weddings out on Long Island. And I believe there's another son as well."

"Do you know anything about this guy Marchbank, the second in command at the Three-G outfit? I remember that he was quoted in the papers after Pierce's death, demanding that the police find the killer immediately if not sooner, or words to that effect."

"You would get an argument from Laura Cordwell over who was number two in the organization."

"Do I smell a rivalry?"

Lily took a sip of coffee and gingerly set her cup in its saucer. "You do indeed. From my sources, I understand that Marchbank, who held the title of assistant executive director, was constantly frustrated because he felt Laura blocked his access to Pierce."

"She obviously possesses something Marchbank lacks."

"Very funny, Mr. Goodwin, I get it."

"Okay, so subtlety has never been my strong suit. Have you met this Marchbank?"

She nodded and pursed her lips. "Only once. Audra introduced us at a luncheon at the Sherry-Netherland. He's not much to look at: short, dark-haired, and wearing what seems to be a permanent scowl. And from that brief time, I felt he had the personality to match his scowl. Later I learned that's pretty much the way he is all the time: sour, sarcastic, sullen. The man is a lawyer, and just as Pierce was leveraging Three-G as a stepping-stone to political office, Marchbank was trying to use his own position to take over as head of Three-G. Like Pierce, Marchbank comes from wealth himself.

"His grandfather made a bundle in gold mining out west years ago, and the family fortune is said to be substantial."

"Since you have such good connections, do you think Mr. Marchbank will end up getting the top job at the Good Government Group, or will that go to the beauty queen?"

"I really don't know, Archie. My sources aren't everywhere."

"So you say. What can you tell me about the lovely Laura?"

"I assume your interest is purely professional?"

"Dare you even ask?"

"Oh, I dare ask, all right, knowing your eye for comely lasses, and Laura Cordwell is indeed comely. She also is probably better suited to run the organization. As was the case with Marchbank, I only met her once at a party, and we talked amicably for several minutes. That was enough to see that she's loaded with tact and charm, both of which Marchbank lacks. And, oh yes, there are those looks of hers as well. But who gets the top spot will really be up to Weldon Dunagan."

"Yeah, the grocery baron; so he calls the shots?"

"Absolutely. The story goes that without him, there would not even be a Good Government Group. He is said to be its largest contributor by far."

"Hardly good news for Inspector Cramer," I said.

"Oh? And why is that?"

I told her the story of Cramer having broken up a brawl involving Dunagan's son, Kevin, years ago and later testifying against the young man in court. I also mentioned the elder Dunagan's profane vow to see Cramer tossed off the force.

"I guess I had forgotten about that, if I even remembered it happening," Lily said. "You are right—this is not good for the inspector, particularly with the clout that Weldon Dunagan has in the so-called corridors of power. Whatever became of the prodigal son?"

"He served some time and now works for Daddy in the family grocery business."

"That is certainly one way of finding employment with a prison record," Lily observed dryly.

"As far as I know, Kevin Dunagan, who was an only child, has sinned no more, or at least he hasn't committed any sin worthy of more time in a jail cell. So I suppose one would have to say he has paid his debt to society."

"I have never met the young man, so I really have no comment," Lily said.

"But you have met several of the others who were close to Pierce, and I have not. Do you have any thoughts as to who might have wanted him dead?"

"Well, wouldn't it figure to be a mob hit? Some of the papers have strongly suggested that, and in the past the syndicate has been known to gun down its enemies from passing cars. And Pierce certainly qualified as an enemy of the mob, the way Three-G has relentlessly gone after them."

"A definite possibility, of course. I was just looking for other options."

"I really don't know who else would qualify as a suspect. Okay, so he was fooling around with the former Miss Missouri, but is that really enough reason for Audra having him shot? I don't believe so. She apparently had tolerated his numerous escapades in the past."

"Do you think the beauty queen was a gold digger, entranced by Lester Pierce's wealth?"

"Hardly, Archie. She came from money herself. Her father is said to be one of the richest men in Missouri. His money comes from banking, so I've heard."

"What about this? Maybe Pierce had grown tired of Laura Cordwell and was dumping her, so she had him bumped off."

Lily brushed my comment away with a well-manicured hand. "Oh, nonsense! You men always seem to think women go all goofy when they are discarded. If anything, it would have been Laura who showed Lester Pierce the door. But in the unlikely event he did happen to cut the romantic ties with her, do you really think she would have any trouble finding someone else?"

"I can't comment because I have never met her."

"But you are dying to, right?"

"I didn't say so."

Lily laughed. "Okay, I will let that one rest for now. Going way back to your original question, I simply cannot imagine who, other than the mob, would want Pierce dead. Now I have a question for you: Just why is the inspector in such hot water now? Earlier you said Pierce's shooting was what *apparently*— your word—got my Dutch uncle in the soup. But over the years, he has survived all sorts of crises and has continued to run the Homicide Squad. Why would this situation be so much different? Is there something else going on?"

"I must be more careful with my language," I said with a grin. "Okay, you've got me. There is speculation—and it is just speculation as far as I know—that Cramer has gotten cozy with the mob."

"More nonsense!" she said, loud enough that diners at two tables turned toward us.

"I know that sounds unlikely, but the inspector has been seen dining with Ralph Mars."

"I haven't read or heard anything about that. This sounds like a tidbit you got from Lon Cohen," Lily said. "How much credibility do you think the story has?"

"I really don't know, but the place where they were said to be seen together is a popular red-checked tablecloth spot in Little Italy for very private chats."

"I still think it's preposterous."

"I am not about to argue, although if that meeting happens to have occurred, I hope the word does not get out. Right now, Cramer has all the trouble he can handle. It is bad enough that Commissioner O'Hara has it in for him because he's a holdover from Skinner's days running the department, and as I'm sure you are aware, O'Hara hates Skinner."

"I wish there were a way for you and Nero Wolfe to do something," Lily said.

"I do too, but as things stand, we sit on the sidelines, and it seems we are likely to stay there."

CHAPTER 6

Days passed with no new developments in the Pierce shooting. Like so many other newspaper stories that start out on page one with bold and breathless headlines followed by exclamation points, this one gradually receded farther toward the back of all the city's daily newspapers, muscled aside by fires, garbage workers' strikes, local government corruption, show-business antics, and, of course, other murders, these involving victims far less well known than Lester Pierce.

One killing that caught my eye was back in the second section of the *Gazette*, headlined "Hit Man Hit!" The short article reported that "Guido Capelli, a reputed mob triggerman, was found shot, execution-style, in the early hours this morning on a side street near the docks in Brooklyn's Red Hook neighborhood. Police said he died from a single gunshot fired at close range to the back of the head. Capelli had been a suspect in several gangland killings over the last several years but had never been convicted of any of the murders. No witnesses have come forth, according to a police spokesman."

Nero Wolfe rarely compliments me; that is not his style. But he once remarked that "upon occasions, albeit rare, you have exhibited a certain amount of presentiment."

"I guess that's nice," I replied. "But what does it mean?"

"It means you get hunches," he said. "Not all of them have significance, of course, but infrequently, you have shown flashes of inspiration." From Wolfe, that constitutes a compliment.

I don't know if I got a flash of inspiration from that brief article in the *Gazette*, but it spurred me to telephone Lon Cohen.

"Didn't you very recently accuse me of calling you on a daily basis?" Lon snapped. "Now it looks like I am going to find myself on the receiving end."

"I haven't started calling you every day—not yet, anyway. But I do have a question."

"Of course you do. Why should I expect anything less?"

"You had a short piece in today about a mob hit man getting a dose of his own medicine over in Red Hook."

"Yeah, and that was a pretty snappy headline, don't you think? 'Hit Man Hit!' You would think we were trying to show the *Daily News* that they are by no means the only ones who get cute with their headlines."

"All right, mark me down as impressed. I have a thought about this."

"You, having thoughts?" Lon shot back. "I thought that was Nero Wolfe's job on the team. You are supposed to be the man of action."

"Okay, okay. Do you happen to know anything about this guy Capelli's modus operandi as a hit man?"

"Modus operandi, is it? Some of Wolfe's vocabulary really has rubbed off on you, Archie."

"Maybe so. Anyway, I'll rephrase the question in language you can understand. Did Capelli have a preferred way of killing his victims?"

"I haven't the foggiest idea," Lon said. "The guy was never convicted of a syndicate killing, although it was common knowledge that he had been a triggerman on more than one occasion. He only served jail time once several years back for being the wheelman in a bank robbery in Queens that went wrong. Why are you so interested?"

"Doesn't it strike you as odd that soon after what looks like the mob murder of Lester Pierce, a mobster gets himself executed?"

"Not particularly. The syndicate has been known to eliminate one of its own on many occasions, and for all sorts of reasons. Job security is not among the strong suits where mob membership is concerned. It seems to me that you are obsessing over what happened to Pierce, at least in part because it has forced Inspector Cramer into what may end up being his permanent retirement. Are you suggesting that this Capelli was Pierce's killer, and then he got silenced because his bosses figured he might blab?"

"Does that really sound so far-fetched?"

"Okay, I suppose not," Lon conceded, "but how in heaven's name could you or anyone else prove any of this? How many times can you think of that a syndicate killing has been solved? The answer to that, which you know as well as I do, is . . . none, zero, naught."

"Well, in the unlikely event that any of your bulldog reporters learn details about how Capelli met his fate, I would appreciate a call."

"I am sure you would. Likewise, if you ever have anything at all to tell me about your interest—or should I say Nero Wolfe's interest—in the unfortunate death of one Lester Pierce, I would be more than happy to hear from you."

"As in, you scratch my back and I scratch yours?"

"If you must put it that way," Lon said, "assuming that is simply a figure of speech."

"Consider it as such," I replied, wondering if we would ever have any information to pass along to each other, either about Capelli's killing or the Pierce murder and Inspector Cramer's real or imagined involvement in it. I felt some kind of action on my part was called for, so in lieu of any other steps, I dialed Saul Panzer.

Saul is a freelance operative we often use, although that description hardly does him justice. He commands double the market rate for non-agency operatives, and even at that he may be undervaluing himself. He is able to sniff out clues better than a bloodhound, and he can hold a tail better than anyone I've ever seen, in part given his ability to blend into the scenery. We both were tailing the same guy one time, and I never spotted Saul, yet he was the one who never lost sight of our prey.

Saul's appearance belies his skills. He's about five feet seven, and he tips the scales at somewhere around 140 pounds after a big meal. His face is about two-thirds nose, but his gray eyes are a far more important feature—they miss nothing. Nero Wolfe puts it best when he says he trusts Saul "more than might be thought credible."

Saul is equally loyal to Wolfe and has been known to drop whatever else he is working on if he's needed on a case at West Thirty-Fifth Street.

We did not have a case at the moment, of course, but I like to anticipate the possibilities, which was why I was calling Saul, who answered "Yeah?" on the first ring.

"What can I do for you, Archie?" he said in that unmistakable Brooklyn accent of his. This despite his having resided on the Manhattan side of the East River for most of his adult life.

"That remains to be seen," I told him. "I have always been impressed by your wide-ranging network of contacts."

"Why do I feel that I am being buttered up?"

"I'm serious, old friend. You know all sorts of people, some of whom live, shall we say, on the fringes of society."

"Pretty fancy talk. I sense what you are trying to say in your quaint way is that I have crossed paths with some individuals who tend to shy away from the limelight, right?"

"I suppose that's one way of putting it."

"Okay, now that we've established where this discussion is heading, what is it that you—or is it Mr. Wolfe—need to know?"

"In this case it's me. Have you read about the Capelli killing?"

"Yes, just what the newspapers carried, which wasn't much."

"Do you know any more about it than what you have read?"

"I don't, Archie, but it sounds like a case of the mob getting rid of one of its own, hardly an unusual occurrence. It happens all the time."

"Do you think by utilizing some of those people of yours who avoid the limelight, you might be able to learn more about the demise of poor Mr. Capelli?"

"Have you asked our mutual friend and fellow poker player, the esteemed Mr. Cohen?"

"In all fairness to Lon, you have better sources than he does."

"I guess I should be flattered," Saul said. "May I be so bold as to inquire about your interest in this? Is it connected in some way to the gunning down of Lester Pierce?"

"It might be."

"Aha. And Mr. Pierce's killing has cast a pall over the long career of one Inspector Cramer of the Homicide Squad. Do I begin to see a pattern forming here?"

"Let me lay my cards on the table for you," I said, "which won't be anything new, as you always seem to know exactly what I'm holding in our weekly games. First off, we have not been hired to investigate the Pierce murder or anything connected with it. At the moment, we are clientless, and possibly clueless as well. Whatever you think, Wolfe seems to have little or no interest in Cramer's difficulties, saying that the inspector can take care of himself, which may very well be true. The man has survived attacks from inside and outside the department before."

"I agree. So you are really on your own here, is that it, playing some sort of hunch?"

"I suppose so. You and I and Wolfe all have this in common: sometimes, we each get an itch that needs to be scratched."

"And your itch is that you need to know why this character Capelli got gunned down mob-style, because it might have something to do with what happened to Mr. Pierce, and what happened to Mr. Pierce has made life extremely uncomfortable for Cramer."

"You have seen right through me."

"Of course I have. All right, I can't guarantee that I'll learn anything, but I will shake a few trees and see what kind of fruit falls out of them," Saul said.

"I'm not looking for a gratis job on your part," I told him. "I will of course pay your standard rates."

"I could be insulted by that, Archie, although knowing you, I realize that you meant well. Your boss, and by extension, you, have thrown so much business my way over the years that I can never repay that."

"I confess to being chagrined."

"That was not my intent. I assume that either Mr. Wolfe already knows about your appeal to me or that you will tell him."

"You have my word that he will be fully informed."

"Good. Before I go out to shake some trees and see what— or who—falls out, I have to finish a job I'm working on with

Durkin. But we've just about got that one wrapped up." The burly Fred Durkin is another freelance operative we often use, and while he is by no means Saul's equal in smarts or in stealth, he is tough, brave, and dogged. And by the way, he once saved my life.

"I will wait to hear from you," I told Saul, and we ended the call.

When Wolfe came down from the plant rooms that morning, got settled in his chair, and rang for beer, I swiveled to face him. "I just got off the phone with Saul," I said.

"Oh?"

I proceeded to relate our conversation. When I had finished, he threw a scowl my way.

"You have taken advantage of Saul's loyalty and his agreeable nature," he said, "by sending him on what may very well be a fool's errand. He could be otherwise engaged in a profitable endeavor. You know very well that his services are in demand, which is hardly surprising."

"As I said, I offered to pay him."

"Pah!" Wolfe snorted, waving my comment away. "He was understandably insulted. You know him well enough to realize that."

"Okay, you've made your point. I'll call him off."

"That would be to no avail. Once his ship is launched, Saul will not steer it back to port without making a discovery."

"Very poetic," I remarked. "Well, I for one look forward to that discovery."

Wolfe did not reply. His nose was in his latest book, *Inside Africa* by John Gunther.

CHAPTER 7

Three days passed and I had heard nothing from Saul, but I was hardly concerned; I figured he and Fred Durkin took longer than expected to wrap up whatever they were working on. When I finally got a call, it was from Fred.

"Archie, something . . . you and Mr. Wolfe should know," he said, coughing. "It's Saul . . . he's in the hospital . . . Greenpoint in Brooklyn."

I felt a chill, although the office was warm, per Wolfe's specifications. "What's happened?" I said, or may have barked, because Fritz appeared at the office doorway within seconds, looking concerned.

"He called me, Archie. He said that he's all right, but he didn't sound very good on the telephone," Fred continued. "He wanted me to know he had gotten the payment for the job we did for that pawnbroker whose employee was cheating him blind."

"Have you got any idea how Saul ended up in a hospital bed?"

"No, but he did say he was glad we wrapped up the pawnbroker business so fast because he had another job he wanted to get started on. I asked him if there was anything he needed in the hospital, and he told me no and said not to tell anyone he was laid up."

"I'm glad you told me, Fred," I said as we ended the call. I went to the kitchen, where Fritz was preparing lunch. "Is everything all right, Archie?" he asked, the concern still evident on his mug.

"I'm not sure. I've got to leave for a while. It's still three hours until we eat, and I may or may not be back. If Mr. Wolfe asks, tell him I had to run an errand."

I went to Curran's Motors over on Tenth Avenue, where we have garaged our cars for years, and I took the Heron sedan. I much prefer the convertible for city driving, but only when I can have the top down, and this blustery morning argued against that. Traffic was light, so I made it to the Greenpoint Hospital in Brooklyn in just over twenty minutes.

Greenpoint had been a New York City fixture far longer than I'd been around town, and as I looked up at its somber six-story brick façade, I felt the old building was starting to show its age. Inside, however, warmth seemed to permeate the place. A smiling—and very attractive—young woman at the front desk gave me Saul's room number on the third floor, and as I walked down the hall and then rode the elevator, I received smiles and hellos from nurses and orderlies of every shape, size, and age. The hospital must require all its employees to take a charm course.

I got to Saul's room and found the door ajar. He was in the bed nearest the window, his face buried in a book. The bed nearest the door was empty.

"Is that holding your interest?" I asked as I stepped into the room.

Saul turned and looked at me, frowning. "I had a feeling you might show up," he said in a tone that was neither welcoming nor angry. He had a broad bandage around his head, and the bruised right side of his face was the color of an eggplant. "Fred told you, didn't he?"

I nodded. "I would trust that man with my life, but probably not with a secret."

"Yeah, I agree. I wouldn't have called him but I wanted to let him know I got our money from the pawnbroker. He's always short of cash, as you are aware, and I wanted to assure him that some greenbacks would soon be coming his way."

"Enough with Fred. Now what is all this about?" I asked, gesturing at our surroundings.

He shifted in the bed, wincing as he did so. "It's a long story, but first the good news: I finally have this room to myself. The occupant of the other bed, who went home first thing this morning, was an old Irishman who spent the days here humming 'My Wild Irish Rose' and 'Oh, Danny Boy,' and 'Galway Bay.' He's a decent guy, but now I'll never get those damned tunes out of my head."

"Glad to hear he's gone out of your life; now what about your long story?"

Saul took a deep breath, wincing again. "I was doing a little investigating for you, and I got careless."

I cursed. "I was afraid it had something to do with our last phone call."

"Now don't go blaming yourself, Archie. I let my guard down, and now I'm paying for it, although my sawbones says I'll be out of here in two, maybe three days, and by next week, I should be close to normal."

"Are you up to telling me what happened?"

"Why not, even if it makes me look stupid? I've got this source, had him for several years, a sawed-off little bird named

Whitey, even shorter than me, who has drifted through life as a racetrack tout, a carnival barker, and a roller-coaster operator at Coney Island, among God knows how many other things."

"A man of many parts," I observed.

"Yeah, but none of these parts have been very successful, at least not in a financial sense. Anyway, Whitey has always seemed to know a lot about the goings-on of the mob, I believe because he had a brother who had been in on some robberies in Brooklyn and Long Island City some years back."

"Isn't it dangerous to talk about the outfit's activities?"

"Of course it is, but Whitey has always been short of cash—our own Fred Durkin is a fat-cat capitalist by comparison. When I called Whitey and told him what I was interested in, he seemed eager to talk, which should have been a red flag. Anyway, at his suggestion I met him at a bar in Williamsburg. A second red flag should have been the sudden vagueness of his conversation. He was evasive when I pressed him about Pierce's shooting, and he told me that we needed to meet with another man, who he said was named Miller. Whitey said he could tell us exactly what had happened to Pierce and why. So the two of us hopped into a taxi and went off to see this Miller over in Bushwick."

"It sounds like a strange—"

"I know, I know," Saul interrupted me. "I had taken leave of my senses, don't remind me. Whitey directed the cabbie to a block of Myrtle Avenue under the elevated tracks, where, he said, Miller would meet us. We got out of the taxi and went halfway along a dark block where most of the shops were closed.

"Miller—if that really is his name—stepped out of a gangway between two buildings, and Whitey introduced us. Miller was a tall skinny character who seemed nervous. 'I'm positive I wasn't followed,' he said, 'but let's keep out of sight just to be safe.' He motioned us back into the gangway, and that's when I got it from behind at least twice with a sap. I went down and I think I hit my head.

"I must have been almost out, but I heard them talking. Miller said to Whitey, or maybe it was the other way around, 'That poor schlub really thought one of the families was behind it.'"

"I suppose he meant one of the Mafia families," I said.

"You suppose right. They thought I was out cold, of course. What really hurt, maybe even more than my head, was the use of that word."

"Schlub?"

"Do you know any Yiddish, Archie?"

"Very little, and I don't know schlub, although I can hazard a guess that it's not exactly a compliment."

"Most dictionaries would describe it as a yokel, a boor, or a worthless person. I am cut to the quick."

"But you are on the mend, which is the most important thing right now. Anything you need that I can get?"

"Just a return of my pride."

"You'll find that soon enough, probably the next time we play poker and you lighten my wallet, as is invariably the case."

"That's something to look forward to. I suppose you will have to report my opacity to your boss."

"*Opacity?* The two of you speak the same language, and it's one that I have never learned."

That got a chuckle out of Saul, but it was followed by a groan. "Lovin' babe, I've got to take it easy."

"I suppose it is hopeless trying to track down this Whitey, let alone Miller," I said.

"Yeah, I don't even know Whitey's given name, and it's a sure thing *Miller* is an alias. Well, so much for my source, who turned out to be a snake. I can't imagine I'll ever see him again, not that I particularly want to. You're going to have to tell Mr. Wolfe that I failed him."

"This was my idea, not his, and he wasn't wild about it. I can only imagine what he's going to say to me when I get home. But I know he'll be happy that you're going to get out of here in a few days."

"I'll be happy, too. They have been good to me in here, but everyone is so blasted cheerful all the time. It's like they're all taking happy pills."

"Well, I will leave you to their ministrations. See, I know a fancy word or two myself."

"Mark me down as impressed," the patient said as I rose to leave. On my way out into the hallway, I passed a perky and grinning nurse who was coming into the room with a lunch tray. "And how are we this lovely fall day, Mr. Panzer?" she asked. The last I saw of Saul, he was rolling his eyes.

CHAPTER 8

I got back to the brownstone just as Fritz was serving lunch. Wolfe gave me a questioning look as I came to the table, where he already was seated, knife and fork at the ready, about to tackle the spareribs. "I will report later; let's eat!" I said, knowing his iron-fast rule about not discussing business during meals, and I considered what had happened to Saul to be business.

Wolfe held forth on the reasons for the downfall of the Roman Empire as we cleaned our plates and then polished off a dessert of papaya custard. As we settled in the office with coffee, I got another look from Wolfe.

"I saw Saul earlier," I said. "He's in the hospital."

"Indeed?" No one can put more meaning into a single spoken word than Nero Wolfe. In this case, the word he mouthed could be described as indicating curiosity, of course, but also incredulity, frustration, vexation, and anger. I plunged ahead.

"He got worked over on a Brooklyn street a couple of nights ago. He'll be okay and should be released this week."

"Go on," he said icily.

"He was . . . looking into the Pierce killing, as I mentioned to you. He said he had a source who knew a lot about the goings-on of the syndicate." I then gave Wolfe a verbatim account of my conversation with Saul.

He sat without speaking for more than a minute, his face set in a glare. After drawing in a bushel of air and releasing it slowly, he said, "Confound it, can he receive telephone calls?"

"I think so."

"Get him, now!"

After finding the hospital's number in the directory, I dialed and got transferred to Saul's room. I nodded to Wolfe, who picked up his receiver just as the patient answered.

"Saul, this is Nero Wolfe. Is it fatuous of me to ask how you are?"

"Fatuous—no, not at all. Each day is better than the last, and the pain continues to recede. Nice of you to call."

"Archie tells me you will be out of the hospital soon."

"I'm hoping maybe the day after tomorrow or maybe the day after that, if the doc gives the okay. I'm letting him call all the shots."

"Excellent. I would like you to be our dinner guest the day you get released. That is, if you are able to take nourishment."

"Hah! I sure can. The food here isn't all that great, but on the other hand, I am in no position to complain. It's edible, and probably healthy as well. But it would be a fine idea if the kitchen at this place brought in Fritz to teach them a few tricks."

"I do not loan him out," Wolfe said, the folds in his cheeks deepening, which for him is a smile, or so he thinks.

■ ■ ■

Three nights later, our front doorbell rang and I played doorman, as is usually the case. "Come in out of the ozone," I told Saul, who looked better than when I had last seen him. The bandage was off his head, the swelling in his face had gone down, and his skin was almost back to its normal sallow tone.

"I understand there's food to be had here," Saul said, flipping his battered flat cap onto one of the hooks in the hall. He's been making that toss for years and he almost never misses.

Five minutes later, we were seated at the table in the dining room, where Fritz served the first course of onion soup with strong beef stock and dry white vermouth.

"Hospitals are all well and good," Saul was saying. "For one thing, they make us appreciate our lives all the more when we're back on the outside. I have never felt as good as when I walked out of that old brick pile called Greenpoint this morning."

That got Wolfe started on hospitals and their history, both in this country and in Europe. By the time he had finished his exposition, we had learned that a six-bed ward founded in the New York City Almshouse in 1736 later became Bellevue Hospital, and that the institution of the public hospital in the United States grew out of a massive need for the caring of the wounded in the Civil War. And we also got treated to minibiographies of Florence Nightingale and Clara Barton, two pioneers of nineteenth-century medical care.

In the office after dinner, Saul made himself at home in the red leather chair with a snifter of the rare Remisier cognac that gets served to favored dinner guests. Wolfe was seated at his desk with two bottles of chilled beer and a pilsner glass, while I sipped on a scotch and soda.

"You do not appear to be suffering any lasting ill effects from your recent contretemps," Wolfe observed.

"Could have been a helluva lot worse," Saul said. "Oh, I've still got some tender spots, but then, with my stupidity, I probably had that coming to me."

"Archie has related what transpired that unfortunate night in Brooklyn, but I would like to hear a recapitulation from you."

Saul took a sip of Remisier, nodded in approval, and cleared his throat. He then essentially repeated what he had told me as Wolfe leaned back in the reinforced desk chair built to accommodate his seventh of a ton, eyes closed and hands interlaced over his middle mound.

When Saul had finished his narrative, Wolfe blinked. "Did those scapegraces who assaulted you believe they had beaten you unconscious?"

"I think so. I was playing possum at that point, hoping they would take off."

"So when they laughed about you believing that one of the Mafia families was behind Lester Pierce's killing, do you feel they were being serious?"

"Yes, absolutely. I do not think it was said for my benefit."

"Do you have any idea as to the identity of the man called Miller?"

"No, none whatever. Whitey only told me he was someone who knew what, or who, was behind the Pierce murder. Now we know it was a setup aimed at getting me out of the way. I'm still puzzled as to why they didn't just kill me right there, not that I'm complaining, mind you. And I don't even know Whitney's surname, although that's often the case with informers. They like to remain as anonymous as possible—they tend to live longer that way."

"Surely," Wolfe said. "And help yourself to more Remisier. Had this Whitey proven to you in the past that he had intimate knowledge of the crime syndicate?"

"That is a damned good question, and one I should have asked. Previously, I had used him mostly to help me identify petty con artists and burglars. He seemed to have a lot of contacts and hinted that his brother has been in the mob.

"Regarding his knowledge of the city's dark underbelly, he was the one who fingered the pawnshop employee in that case Fred Durkin and I just wrapped up. The bozo we caught was an employee of the shop who had been dipping into the till."

Saul continued. "'That there is good old Lefty Zeller,' Whitey said with a laugh when we looked through the pawnshop's front window from our vantage point in a doorway across the street. 'He's lifted cash or goods from every place he's ever worked. It's truly amazing that he hasn't been caught more often. There's your man, bank on it.' So Durkin and I eventually ended up nailing Zeller, practically in the act. And to think, I gave Whitey a double sawbuck for his help, and I get this in return," Saul said, touching the spot on his temple that still was swollen from the beating.

"Sorry, I got off the track and didn't answer your question," Saul told Wolfe. "Whenever I've used Whitey—it has been a half dozen times now—he always hints as to how he knows a lot about what's going on in the mob, and he mentions enough names of its members, including some of its minor players, to make him sound believable. He sure as hell had me conned. Mark me down as a grade-A chump."

"Do not be too hard on yourself," said Wolfe, who is always willing to give Saul the benefit of the doubt. "Based on what you have told us, there was no reason to believe the man was a turncoat."

"Maybe you are right, but I still feel like a fool."

"We all are fools at one time or another. It is endemic to the human condition."

"Very nice; who said that?" Saul asked.

"I did, although it is likely I picked up the quote along the way," Wolfe replied, flipping a palm. "I believe Laurence Peter gave voice to many of us when he wrote that 'Originality is the fine art of remembering what you hear but forgetting where you heard it.'"

"You are being too modest," Saul said.

"Modest, no, realistic, yes. Let us move on. I know, of course, that Archie was the impetus behind your recent ill-fated expedition, sans any discussion with me. No matter. I find myself becoming increasingly intrigued by the Pierce killing. I have no client, nor do I anticipate one at present. Again, no matter. Has your recent unpleasant experience prejudiced you against any further investigation into the Pierce case?"

"Hell, no, rather the contrary," Saul replied. "Lead me to it."

"Archie?" Wolfe said, swiveling toward me.

"I'm all in, client or no. As you are aware, the bank balance is experiencing good health."

Wolfe drank beer and glared at the empty glass. "I begin with the assumption that the crime syndicate, or the Mafia, or whatever you choose to call this pernicious force, is not responsible for Lester Pierce's death. Do either of you take issue with that position?" We both shook our heads.

"Is Fred Durkin available?" Wolfe asked.

"He is almost always available," Saul said. "Even now, with his wallet fattened by the payday he and I got from that pawnshop business."

"I suggest the four of us meet here tomorrow night, nine o'clock, unless either you or Fred has a pressing engagement."

"If anyone cares, I can make it," I said.

"Me too," Saul put in. "And as for Fred, it's fair to say I can guarantee his presence."

CHAPTER 9

And so it was that twenty four hours later, the four of us gathered in the office, Wolfe at his desk with beer, Saul in the red leather chair and me at my desk, each of us with a scotch, and Fred Durkin in one of the yellow chairs with beer. Fred feels that in Wolfe's presence, he should be drinking what the host consumes.

"Gentlemen," Wolfe said, "thank you for being here tonight. Archie and Saul already know why we have convened, Fred, so it is time to bring you up to speed, to use one of Mr. Goodwin's favorite phrases.

"We are going to investigate the murder of Lester Pierce, although we do not have a client and are unlikely to obtain one. However," Wolfe continued, nodding toward Saul and Fred, "each of you will be reimbursed for your work at your usual rates."

"I'm just curious," Fred said, "and maybe this is none of my business, Mr. Wolfe, but why are you interested in this? And why is there no client?"

I knew the answer, and I'm sure you do as well as you read this: Wolfe was outraged at what had happened to Saul and was determined to avenge the attack on him. But I was intrigued as to how he would respond to the question.

Wolfe downed the first of his two beers and dabbed his lips with a handkerchief he had pulled from his center desk drawer. "You raise valid questions, Fred, and ones that demand an answer. But first, a question for you: How do you feel about George Rowcliff, who now is a captain?"

"The man is a weasel!" Fred barked. "I'd like to take him and—"

"You have made your point forcefully," Wolfe said, holding up a hand, which for him is a strong gesture. "And I agree with your assessment of the gentleman, if he can be so termed. During Inspector Cramer's forced furlough, Mr. Rowcliff also is acting head of the Homicide Squad, as you probably are aware."

"I am," Fred said, grim-faced.

"I believe I speak for all four of us when I say that in any future relations with the New York City Police Department, we would far prefer dealing with Mr. Cramer rather than Mr. Rowcliff. Does anyone disagree with that opinion?" We all shook our heads.

"This is not to say I embrace all of Mr. Cramer's techniques and attitudes, far from it. But he is easily the better alternative. As each of you is aware, he is under a cloud because of the murder of Lester Pierce and the attacks by Pierce on the inspector that were launched by the Good Government Group."

"It seems like Cramer should be able to ride all this out," Saul said. "He has taken a lot of criticism from the press and others many times in the past."

"True, but there is something else the two of you probably don't know," Wolfe replied, looking first at Saul, then at Fred.

"The inspector has been seen dining in a Little Italy restaurant with Ralph Mars."

Saul opened his mouth and probably was about to say "lovin' babe" when Durkin spoke. "There's been nothing in print about this unless I missed it."

"You are correct, Fred," Wolfe said. "But we have this piece of information on good authority."

"Lon Cohen, no doubt," Saul remarked. "And if I were to hazard a guess, the reason that meeting has not been in print is because the news of it came from a *Gazette* source Cohen and others on the paper may feel to be untrustworthy."

"Your guess is more than a guess," Wolfe said. "Now, to respond to Fred's earlier queries: I believe I answered his first question, at least implicitly. I want to remove the cloud that hangs over Inspector Cramer so that he will resume his role as head of the Homicide Squad. As to the second question, no one has come forward as a potential client, although one individual has all but begged us to conduct an investigation. Unfortunately, he lacks the capital I normally require to undertake a case."

"Sounds suspiciously like one Sergeant Purley Stebbins," Saul said.

Wolfe dipped his chin half an inch. "Your recent mishap has not in any way undermined your discernment. How do all of you feel about this undertaking?"

"Anything that might take that blockhead Rowcliff down a few pegs is jake with me," Fred Durkin said. "Sign me up."

"Fred said it better than I could have," Saul added. "I'm ready for my marching orders."

"Who am I to buck the trend?" I put in. "Besides, if my boss says we have a job, I always respond with 'yes, sir.'"

"As I said to Archie and Saul earlier, I begin with the assumption that the crime syndicate was not behind the killing of Mr. Pierce," Wolfe told Fred. "Are you uncomfortable with my belief?"

"No, sir, not if you say so, although it sure seemed like a mob-style hit."

"Such was surely the intent. Continuing with my assumption, does anyone have a theory as to who or what might be behind what the newspapers are terming an 'assassination'?"

"What about someone inside that Good Government Group?" Saul asked. "I don't know a lot about the organization, although I've heard—and read in a couple of the gossip columns—that there was some friction among the leadership."

"Can you be more specific?" Wolfe asked.

"Two people each apparently feel they should take over as Three-G executive director: Roland Marchbank, the assistant executive director, and Laura Cordwell, whose role was in effect as administrative assistant to Pierce, although rumors were that she had, shall we say, a more *personal* relationship with him."

Wolfe made a face. "You are suggesting the Cordwell woman is a Jezebel?"

"I have to confess that I don't know my Bible all that well," Saul replied, "but of course I know who she was, and Miss Cordwell certainly could play the role in a motion picture if the rumors about her have any substance."

"Was Mr. Pierce married?" Wolfe asked.

Saul nodded. "Yes, he had been for many years, to Audra Kingston Pierce, age fifty-five, who comes from money and is involved in a whole slew of charities."

"Lily Rowan has met Mrs. Pierce several times," I put in. "According to Lily, the woman is attractive, although she tends to be arrogant and pleased with herself. But she also is generous in contributing to good causes with both her time and her money. And the word is, she was well aware of her husband's relationship with Laura Cordwell and, for whatever reasons, chose to ignore it."

I went on, "Since we are beginning to sound like gossip columnists, I will throw this in: long before his liaison with Laura Cordwell, Lester Pierce already had a reputation as what Lily refers to as a lothario."

When Fred looked puzzled at that word, I jumped in. "A lothario is a man who . . . well—"

"A man who seduces women," Wolfe interrupted, clearly uncomfortable with the subject matter.

"Yet there was speculation that Pierce, who went by the nickname 'Saint Lester' because of his sanctimonious bearing and his church involvement, had his sights on running for governor one day," I said.

"How could a guy hope to run for a big office like that with that kind of a private life?" Fred asked.

"It has been done before," Saul responded. "Take our long-dead Warren Harding, well-known skirt chaser and father of a child by a woman he wasn't married to. And he made it all the way to the White House. Okay, so he was not much of a president, but my point is that a lack of morality does not necessarily exclude someone from seeking high office if the candidate's sins are not widely publicized—or sometimes even if they are. And it seems that Pierce's lapses, while known in certain quarters, have not made it into print."

"Your point is well taken," Wolfe said. "We tend to glorify our political and business leaders, but many if not most of them have feet of clay in one area or another. We cannot eliminate the possibility that one of Mr. Pierce's lascivious transgressions may have been the cause of his violent demise."

"Okay, so we have to consider that either a wronged woman or a cuckolded husband could have bumped off Pierce," I said.

"And you also remain convinced the killing was not done by the crime syndicate?"

"I do," Wolfe said. "Let us return to this Good Government Group. What else do we know about it?"

"For one thing—and it's a big thing—the Three-G operation is heavily bankrolled by Weldon Dunagan, the multimillionaire grocery chain magnate who detests the syndicate," Saul said. "One would have thought if the mob wanted to bump somebody off, it would be him, not Pierce."

"How did this Dunagan character get along with Pierce?" Fred asked.

"That is a question I could put to Lon Cohen," I said, "but I can only assume they must have hit it off okay, because Pierce had been top dog at Three-G since its inception several years ago. I can't imagine Dunagan would put up with anybody he didn't like or didn't think was doing a good job."

"What constitutes a good job?" Wolfe posed. "After all, this group has, as you say, been around for several years, and what success has it had in battling organized crime? Not a great deal, by all accounts. One of the reasons I do not feel mobsters were behind Mr. Pierce's death is they had little to fear from him and what is essentially his toothless operation."

"Point taken," Saul said. "Where do we go from here?"

"We start by having you unearth everything you can about the essence of the meeting between Inspector Cramer and Ralph Mars at that restaurant in Little Italy," Wolfe told Saul. "It is a difficult assignment, but I trust you will avail yourself of the resources at your disposal."

"I'm on it."

"Fred, we need to learn more about Guido Capelli, the syndicate hit man who himself became the victim of a hit. Why was he killed, was he still a member of the mob, or had he become a rogue, working only for himself? But go forth cautiously, given what happened to Saul when he undertook to find out more about this man."

"I know of some people who might be helpful," Fred said, knitting his broad brow. "And I will be careful." Wolfe's expression told me he was well aware of the man's limitations. As I have mentioned, Fred Durkin takes a backseat to no one in the bravery and loyalty departments, but he is not always the wisest of operatives. However, I was not about to quarrel with Wolfe's decision regarding the assignment.

"Archie, you are to meet with Weldon Dunagan and ascertain his attitudes about Mr. Pierce, both as an executive and an individual. No doubt he will respond to your questions with platitudes about the dead man's sterling character and his admirable work ethic. However, I know you to be a skillful and shrewd interrogator, so you should be able to penetrate Mr. Dunagan's defenses."

If you think Wolfe was buttering me up, you are all aces, but I got used to that approach a long time ago. Also, he did not provide any suggestions as to how I was to obtain an audience with Dunagan, and if I had asked, he would have given me his standard reply: "You are to act in the light of experience as guided by intelligence." Swell.

Wolfe finished his second beer and considered each of us in turn. "Gentlemen, you have your initial assignments, and more may follow. Report your progress to Archie, and he will relay the results to me. I wish you all a good night." He rose and made what he thinks is a bow, walking out of the office to the elevator.

CHAPTER 10

The next morning after breakfast, I settled in at my desk with coffee and flipped through the Manhattan phone directory, finding the Dunagan office on Pine Street, which I knew to be down in the Financial District, an area I rarely frequented.

I dialed and was rewarded with a cultured female saying, "DunaganMart Foods, how may I direct your call?" I told her I wanted to speak to Weldon Dunagan, and she transferred me to another cultured female voice, which informed me that I had reached the executive suite.

"My name is Archie Goodwin, and I work for the private detective Nero Wolfe, of whom you may have heard. I would like to speak to Mr. Weldon Dunagan."

"I am so sorry, Mr. Goodwin, but Mr. Dunagan will be occupied in meetings all day. May I get word to him regarding why you wish to see him?"

"You may. Mr. Wolfe is investigating the death of Lester Pierce."

"I believe that sad occurrence is in the hands of the police," she said. "I am sure Mr. Dunagan would tell you the same thing."

"It is our understanding that Mr. Dunagan is not happy with the way the police department is conducting the investigation, Miss . . . ?"

"It's Mrs. Kirby," she replied, taking on a slightly more cordial tone.

"Well, Mrs. Kirby, I believe Mr. Dunagan will be very interested to learn that someone other than the New York City Police Department is taking an active interest in the heartless murder of one of the city's most respected civic leaders, an individual who I know worked very closely with Mr. Dunagan. I realize how busy your boss must be, and I would be happy to come to his office and discuss the matter with him at his convenience."

That little speech resulted in several seconds of silence on the other end. Finally, Mrs. Kirby spoke. "Please give me your number, Mr. Goodwin, and I will talk to Mr. Dunagan when I can catch him in a free moment."

"You would not just be putting me off now, would you, Mrs. Kirby?" I said in what I hoped was a friendly voice.

"No, Mr. Goodwin, I would not," she replied in a neutral tone. "I happen to have known—and liked—Mr. Pierce myself, as he met here with Mr. Dunagan several times on Good Government Group matters. He was a fine gentleman, and I am sure I feel as strongly as Mr. Dunagan that his murderer must be caught."

"Well said. When am I likely to hear from you or Mr. Dunagan?"

"I promise that you will receive a call from someone this morning, even if that someone happens to be me."

"It would not bother me in the least if it happened to be you, Mrs. Kirby."

■ ■ ■

At 10:15 a.m., the phone rang. "I managed to corral Mr. Dunagan between meetings, and he said he could give you a few minutes at one o'clock," Mrs. Kirby said. "I hope that time is suitable for you."

I told her it was, not bothering to mention that I would have to miss lunch in the brownstone. But then, such sacrifices sometimes had to be made, at least by me, although rarely if ever by Wolfe.

Following Mrs. Kirby's directions, I entered a glass-and-stone skyscraper in the man-made canyons of Lower Manhattan and rode an elevator to the forty-fourth floor. The doors of the elevator opened onto a carpeted lobby big enough to hold a tennis court. On one wall, silver foot-high capital letters spelled out DUNAGAN INTERNATIONAL.

Other walls were graced with framed photographs of the exteriors and interiors of DunaganMarts in this country and around the world, along with a head and shoulders oil portrait of the white-haired Weldon Dunagan, wearing a pin-striped suit and a tight smile.

If I was supposed to be impressed with the surroundings, it worked, at least to a degree. I walked thirty feet across thick carpeting to a mahogany-and-chromium reception desk where a well-coiffed brunette with a turned-up nose gave me a smile that showed off the artistry of an orthodontist. "May I help you, sir?"

All I had to do was give Dunagan's name as well as my own, and she quickly picked up a white telephone that had no dial. "Mr. Goodwin is here," she spoke, then gently cradled the instrument. Less than a half minute later, a tall, slender woman of a certain age, also well coiffed, emerged from a door to the right of the front desk.

"Mr. Goodwin, so nice to meet you; I am Carolyn Kirby," she said, holding out a slender hand, which I took. She was no slouch in the smile department herself, with a grin that would have lit up a funeral parlor, although she clearly was older than her telephone voice had suggested. I followed her down a long hall to a set of paneled double doors at the end.

Carolyn Kirby rapped lightly on one of the twin doors and pulled it open, revealing an office with windows on two sides that, while smaller than the lobby, was still larger than almost any living room or parlor I had ever set foot in. A broad-shouldered Weldon Dunagan, clad in a double-breasted, pin-striped suit similar to the one in his portrait, worked at an oversize cherry-wood desk that was set on a diagonal in the far corner.

Carolyn gestured me to one of a pair of chairs in front of the desk and silently made her exit. Dunagan did not acknowledge my presence as he continued signing a stack of correspondence. He was sending a clear message that his time was more precious than mine. Given his income, he was correct.

After signing the last of the documents, he carefully screwed the top on his fountain pen and slid it into his breast pocket, then looked up. "Mr. Goodwin," he said, fixing ice-blue eyes on me, "first, you should know this: I have little or no use for private detectives."

"So noted, Mr. Dunagan."

"However, I have even less use for most police officers, particularly the ones who are presumably trying to learn who killed Lester Pierce. My general attitude about the police is part of the reason I recently agreed to become a member of the Police Review Board. So when Mrs. Kirby told me that your Nero Wolfe—whom I happen to have heard of, although I can't remember where—was looking into the case, I agreed to see you. Has Wolfe managed to learn anything yet?"

"He has just begun his investigation," I responded.

"Is that the standard private eye's response to questions about progress in a case?" Dunagan demanded.

"Responses vary. The reason I am here is to ask if you have any thoughts as to who would want Mr. Pierce dead."

"Hah! I, of course, got asked that obvious question by the thickheaded Captain George Rowcliff, who is acting head of the Homicide crew. Do you know him?"

"We have met."

Dunagan sneered. "The police desperately need brighter people, but then, that's always been obvious. Cramer was running that operation, but he got pushed aside. Good riddance."

"I have always had the impression that Mr. Cramer was well regarded," I deadpanned.

"You obviously don't know a lot about the inspector's history, Mr. Goodwin. I will just leave it at that. Back to your original question—who would want Lester dead? The crime syndicate, of course. That's patently clear to damned near everyone. I think the police department is afraid to take them on. What about your boss—is he afraid of those thugs too?"

"I have worked for Mr. Wolfe for a long time, and there are very few people he has ever been afraid of. Let's get back to Lester Pierce. I'm sure you knew him very well. Are you aware if he had made enemies other than in the mob?"

"As far as I am aware, Lester led an exemplary life—family man, churchgoer, fighter against injustice and particularly against organized crime. It would be hard to imagine this could have been anything other than a mob hit."

I had to wonder how well Dunagan really knew Lester Pierce, but I pushed ahead. "Did his staff seem to relate well to him and his leadership?"

"Of course they did—what a question! Why wouldn't they? The man was a born leader."

"I am simply exploring every avenue. I understand you are by far the biggest contributor to the Good Government Group. Does that mean you will be the one who selects Mr. Pierce's successor?"

"I find that to be impudent!" Dunagan fixed a glare at me, one that probably had intimidated others sitting in my chair.

"Impudent, why?" I said with a shrug. "Because of your strong financial commitment to the organization, I simply assumed you want to ensure that it has capable direction going forward."

That threw him off. "Well . . . of course I want to see Three-G remain in good hands. That goes without saying. I believe Roland Marchbank is fully capable of steering the ship, so to speak."

"Our sources tell us Laura Cordwell also has her eyes on the top job."

"And just who are your sources, Mr. Goodwin?" Dunagan demanded, red-faced and with a vein throbbing in his neck.

"I am not at liberty to say, but I can assure you they are reliable."

"By God, I have had enough of you and your insolence!" Dunagan said, standing and pushing a button on his desk. "Mrs. Kirby will show you out."

"I am very surprised, Mr. Dunagan, that you do not seem concerned about what is going on in a civic group you have done so much to foster." I rose to leave just as Carolyn Kirby stepped into the room, her face a question mark.

"Mr. Goodwin is leaving," Dunagan said between deep breaths. "Hold all my calls until you hear from me."

I grinned at the lady as she held the door for me, her expression still reflecting puzzlement.

"I must say I'm glad for the opportunity to have met you," I told her. "I am only sorry we did not have the opportunity to chat. I believe we both would have found the experience educational."

I looked over my shoulder to take one last look at Weldon Dunagan, who had his head down, apparently studying a sheet of paper on his desk. As far as he was concerned, I had ceased to exist.

CHAPTER 11

"You would not like him one iota," I told Wolfe in the office after my meeting with Dunagan.

"I did not expect to, based on what I have read and heard about the man. Report," he said, drinking from the first of two chilled beers Fritz had placed before him after his descent from the plant rooms that afternoon.

"I don't think I penetrated Dunagan's defenses, as you suggested I might be able to do, but here it is." I then gave him the verbatim of our conversation, hardly a challenge for me because of its brevity. When I finished, he sat with his eyes closed for a full minute. When he opened them, he said, "We have not heard from either Saul or Fred." No sooner had he spoken than the phone rang, as if on cue.

It was Saul, and I motioned for Wolfe to pick up his receiver. "It's good to know people who know people," he said to us. "I was surprised at just how quickly I was able to be put in touch with someone who was present at the dinner between Ralph

Mars and Inspector Cramer. Of course it helps to spread a few dollars around in the right places."

"You will be reimbursed," Wolfe said.

"Oh, I am not in the least worried about that," Saul replied. "I know where Archie keeps the petty cash. Anyway, I don't want to oversell the importance of what I've come up with. For the record, my source is an underpaid restaurant employee who very possibly is in this country without the necessary documentation. He clearly recalls that dinner meeting between Mars and a man he described in detail to me."

"A man who happens to bear a striking resemblance to a longtime police inspector?" I asked.

"You catch on fast. You may find that you have a future as an operative. My source had occasion to visit their back corner table several times to refill water glasses, bring more bread, and do the other things expected of a busboy. 'Mr. Mars comes in often,' he told me, 'and this time he was with a man I had never seen before. They were talking very quietly, with their heads close together like they were telling secrets to each other.'

"When I asked the busboy if he had heard any of the content of their conversation, he said one word kept coming up. 'Peerze,' he told me. 'They said Peerze to each other, more times than once, but that was all that I could understand. Will you still pay me?'

"Of course I gave him something—a double sawbuck to be specific—but I didn't learn anything else from him, and I wasn't surprised, since his English is none too good. So as I said earlier, I don't want to oversell what I got."

"Satisfactory," Wolfe replied, which for him amounts to high praise. But then, in his eyes, Saul can do no wrong.

After we had hung up, I turned to Wolfe. "Any thoughts?"

"If nothing else, it appears we now know the subject of the unlikely parley."

"Yeah, but just where does this put us?"

"Perhaps we will learn more when Fred reports," Wolfe said, but his tone was less than enthusiastic.

In fact, Fred Durkin did have some success with his assignment. He phoned us that evening, a few minutes before we went in to dinner. "Archie, I found out a few things about this Capelli character from this, uh . . . acquaintance of mine."

"Is this someone whose name you want to share with us?" I asked as Wolfe picked up his instrument.

"Not really, Archie. Do you have to know?"

"This is Nero Wolfe. Do you consider this source to be reliable?"

"Yes, sir, I do. Over the years, he has been well, involved in—"

"That is enough, Fred. Go on," Wolfe said.

"Yes, sir. It turns out that Capelli had a reputation within the mob as something of a rogue."

"Meaning that he didn't always follow orders from the boys on high?" I asked.

"That's right. He had established himself as a dependable hit man, all right, but sometimes he freelanced for people who were outside the organization, and his bosses did not like that one bit. He had been warned to cut it out, but he liked the cash he was making from these 'side jobs' of his."

"Did your source suggest Mr. Capelli was behind Lester Pierce's killing?" Wolfe asked.

"Yeah, he more than suggested it; he said it was a fact."

"Did this person know who had hired Capelli to kill Mr. Pierce?"

"He said he didn't, and I believe him. All he claimed to know was that whoever this was, he—or I suppose it could have been a she—seemed to know Pierce."

"So because he was freelancing, the syndicate had Capelli killed, is that the story?" I asked.

"I really don't know, Archie," Fred answered. "My source said he wasn't sure who did Capelli in. From what my guy knew about the murder, he said it had the look of a mob job, but he pointed out that it isn't unusual for somebody to make a shooting appear like the outfit was behind it so that they are the ones who end up getting the blame."

"That is a smart move," I said, "because none of those mob killings ever get solved anyway."

"Did your source have anything else to contribute?"

"That's about it, Mr. Wolfe. At first, he didn't even want to talk to me, but I was forced to remind him that I once got him out of a tight jam."

"Did you have need to pay him?"

"No, sir, that reminder was more than enough to loosen his tongue."

"Very well, Fred. We may be seeking your services again regarding the death of Lester Pierce. And you will be reimbursed for your time and efforts."

"Thank you, Mr. Wolfe. I am always available."

After the call had ended, I turned to Wolfe. "Saul and Fred have some interesting sources, don't they?"

"Yes, and sources whose anonymity they choose to protect, a stance that is both prudent and, in the long run, beneficial, both to us and to them."

"Agreed. As you are aware, I also know a few people around town who have been helpful to us over the years, and even you do not know the names of most of them."

"I prefer to keep it that way," Wolfe said.

"I agree again. Back to business, what's next?"

He drank beer, licked his lips, and glanced at the wall clock. "We, of course, go to the dining room for breaded fresh pork tenderloin. We certainly do not want to keep Fritz waiting."

CHAPTER 12

After dinner, in the office with coffee, I waited for Wolfe to continue our premeal discussion, but he seemed in no hurry. As he uncapped one of the two beers before him and reached for his book, I finally broke the silence. "Got an assignment for me? I'm able-bodied, eager, and chomping at the bit. Or should it be champing at the bit?"

"Both usages are correct," Wolfe said, setting the book down and sighing, as if he were being put upon. "See Miss Cordwell, get to know her, learn her attitudes toward Messrs. Pierce and Marchbank and her expectations about her future with the Good Government Group. And of course, ask who she thinks might have dispatched Mr. Pierce. I trust you will not find the assignment to be onerous."

Years ago, Wolfe got it into his head that I have a talent for beguiling attractive women and getting them to spill their deepest secrets to me. I have suggested on numerous occasions that he grossly overestimates my charm, but he remains convinced of my persuasive abilities with the female species.

"All right, I will tackle the lady, figuratively, of course. But please bear in mind that she possesses a master's degree from one of our great universities, while my own higher education, if it can be so termed, consists of but a few weeks at a small Ohio college."

That evoked another sigh. "I am sure you will find ways to bridge the academic chasm that separates you," Wolfe said. With that, he opened his book and disappeared behind it, ending the discussion.

And of course, in truth, it did not in the least bother me that Laura Cordwell's educational credentials far outstripped mine. I have never regretted my lack of postsecondary schooling, given that what I have learned in what some call the "college of hard knocks" more than compensates for any lack of time spent in some ivy-covered joint with robed professors who possess multiple degrees.

I merely went on at length about education to get Wolfe away from his book and concentrate on the case. Part of the reason he hired me was to be a burr under his saddle. The man can be lazy—he has admitted it—and I find it necessary on occasion to steer him back to the business at hand at the risk of irritating him.

The next morning, I telephoned the Good Government Group's offices on Lexington Avenue and was informed by a youthful-sounding male that Laura Cordwell was in meetings and might very well be tied up all day.

"I believe she will want to see me," I told him. "I am part of a team of investigators looking into the death of Mr. Pierce."

"I will tell her, sir," the man said, taking my name and number. Less than an hour later, the phone rang.

"Mr. Goodwin, this is Laura Cordwell of the Good Government Group. Charlie gave me your message, and I must say I have no idea who you are or who you represent. As you can appreciate, I already have had several conversations with police officers. And I found it interesting that your message did not specify what type of investigator you are."

"A private one, Miss Cordwell, albeit duly licensed by the great state of New York. I work for Nero Wolfe. You may have heard of him."

"I have," she said after a pause. "Just what is it you hope to learn where the police have been unsuccessful, at least thus far?"

"I am not sure yet, and please understand that Mr. Wolfe and I are not in competition with the police department. However, there are situations in which we may have an advantage over law enforcement agencies."

"Is that so? I should like to hear more about that so-called advantage you and your colleague have."

"I would be glad to discuss the matter with you—in person, Miss Cordwell."

"You are a persistent sort, aren't you?" she said in a tone that I took to be both irritable and mildly curious.

"I have been called far worse. But I also know you are a person of intelligence, grace, and charm."

"And where, pray tell, have you heard that, Mr. Goodwin? Your attempt to flatter me is sadly transparent."

"Oh, I am sorry you think so. I was merely passing along an impression of you that I got from an acquaintance of mine named Lily Rowan."

"Lily? She and I had the most interesting conversation a while back at a party. What a lady. I'm so glad I met her. She is . . . a friend of yours?"

"A very good friend, Miss Cordwell. If you have any reluctance to see me because of your concern about my character, my profession, or my social graces, please give Lily a call. I know her number.

I am taking a risk, of course, because she may tell you things about me that I would rather not have known. For instance, I am unable to carry a tune, I have been known to yell too loudly at a Rangers game when they do something stupid, and I occasionally snore."

"And who told you that?"

"I have no comment. Would you like Lily's number? I have it memorized."

"I am sure you do. I remember now that when she and I were talking, she mentioned a friend who she often went dancing with. Do you by any chance happen to be a good dancer, Mr. Goodwin?"

"Modesty forbids me from responding."

"Of course it does. How silly of me for even bothering to ask. Can you be at our offices at three o'clock today?"

"I can. Should I bring flowers?"

"Not necessary. I trust you know where we are located."

"I do. I will make sure my shoes are shined for the occasion and that I brush my teeth and my hair."

"I should hope so."

At 2:55 p.m., I entered a nondescript and aging office building on an equally nondescript block of Lexington and took the elevator to the fourth floor. To call the reception area of the Good Government Group shabby might be a bit harsh, but the room had seen better days and needed a fresh coat of paint—on the ceiling as well as the walls.

Behind a desk, a long-faced young man who could use some meat on his bones smiled and nodded at me, eyebrows raised. "I am here to see Miss Cordwell. My name is Goodwin," I replied to his unspoken question.

"Yes, sir, it was me that you talked to earlier. She is expecting you. Her office is the second door on the right behind me.

Go right in, I will tell her you are here," he said, picking up his telephone.

I don't like barging in on anyone, even when I am expected, so I rapped lightly on the drab door marked LAURA CORDWELL and heard "come in."

The former beauty queen was seated behind an unadorned wood desk with a window behind her that looked out on a Chinese restaurant, a women's shoe store, and a shop with a red neon sign that blinked the words ADULT BOOKS. It wasn't the outside view that caught my eye but rather the former Miss Missouri, a brunette with high cheekbones, large blue eyes, and a dazzling smile.

"Mr. Goodwin, how nice to meet you," she said, sounding genuine. She stood and held out a hand, which I took. Her grip was firm as she gestured me to a chair in front of her desk.

"Now, sir, you have finagled—and skillfully, I must admit— to have this meeting. Well, the floor is yours; please proceed. I am all ears, as they say."

"All right, Miss—"

"Before you go any further, please call me Laura. We are not big on formality here."

"Thank you. And I go by Archie. You said on the telephone that you have heard of my boss."

"Nero Wolfe? Yes, of course. Although I am not a native New Yorker—I have been here only eight years, and that includes my time as a graduate student—I know that I have seen his name in the newspapers on several occasions. But not yours, I am afraid to say."

"He is the brains of our operation and deserves all the credit. I'm just a guy running around behind the scenes trying to follow his orders."

"And in this particular situation, just what are the orders you have been given, Mr. Archie Goodwin?" she asked, folding her arms over her chest.

"One, to learn about the workings of the Good Government Group, and two, to discover why someone would have a reason to shoot Lester Pierce."

"I can be of some help with the first of those tasks you have been given, but I am afraid I will be of less help to you on the second."

"Fair enough. Tell me about the organizational structure of Three-G. Or is it sacrilege to refer to it in that way?"

She laughed. It was a nice laugh. "No, not at all. This place is anything but stuffy, I assure you. We do important work, Archie, but I think it is fair to say that we don't take ourselves too seriously."

"I'm glad to hear that. Back to my question," I said with a smile.

"Of course, I had not forgotten. As I am sure you know, our organization was the brainchild of Lester Pierce, who had been appalled at the growing and unchecked power of the local crime syndicate. He had long felt that neither the police nor the press was doing as much as they could to combat the spread of organized crime in New York."

"His position is hard to quarrel with, but how successful has the Good Government Group really been?"

"For one thing, under Lester's leadership these last several years, we have met with the top editors of every one of the city's daily newspapers and urged them to step up their coverage of the mob and demand that the police put the squeeze on the syndicate. Several of the papers, particularly the *Times*, *News*, and *Gazette*, have run strong editorials urging the police to get tougher on the syndicate. And although I have no way of proving it, I believe these editorials were a direct result of the meetings we had with the editors and publishers. We also have on numerous occasions sat down with the police commissioner and several of his top officers."

"How would you say those meetings went?"

Laura raised her shoulders and let them drop slowly. "Mixed, at best. All of us—Lester, Roland Marchbank, and me—felt that Commissioner O'Hara was being patronizing to us, as if we were naive and childlike and needed to be lectured. He would say things like 'You have no idea how difficult it is to make charges against these people stick.' Then he would suggest in an indirect way that even when the police did make arrests of syndicate figures, the district attorney's office would be unable to deliver convictions."

"Do you think O'Hara is in league with the syndicate?"

"Oh no, no, Archie. I did not for a moment mean to suggest that," she said, leaning forward in her chair. "I have no reason whatever to doubt the commissioner's honesty."

"How do you feel about the other top cops?"

"I think Inspector Cramer is probably the best of the bunch, although I understand that he is on some sort of administrative leave right now, and I have no idea what that's about. He has always seemed to take our concerns seriously."

"What about George Rowcliff?"

She stiffened and fixed me with a firm, unblinking gaze. "I am trying to decide how trustworthy you are."

"Meaning you believe I might take anything you tell me and run to the police or the press with it?"

"No . . . I don't mean that," she said in a voice just above a whisper, her face coloring. "It's just that I don't want to have things I say used against me."

"Well, I am not sure how I can reassure you about my discretion. For starters, you could ask Lily Rowan. Many times I've been involved in a case, and she has asked me about details—simply because she's curious by nature—and I have clammed up. Beyond that, I can only say I have been a private investigator in this town for years, and if I had been a blabbermouth, I would have been shipped back to the hills of southern Ohio long ago."

That brought the trace of a smile. "For some reason, I believe you. Could it be your native charm?"

"Once again, I refer you to Miss Rowan."

She laughed. "All right, let us say you have won your point. None of us here have been the least bit impressed with Captain Rowcliff. Off the record, I think he likes to hear himself talk."

"On or off the record, I second that opinion. And if you think I am not a fan of the gentleman, you should hear what my boss has to say about him."

"That doesn't sound very discreet of you, Archie."

"Nero Wolfe would not object to my saying it. And now if you don't mind, I would like to shift gears away from the police."

"Shift away."

"You said earlier that you didn't feel you would be of much help on the subject of who shot Mr. Pierce. You can think of no possible killers?"

"I suppose the standard answer would be the crime syndicate, but that does not seem likely to me. For one thing, Three-G has not put them out of business, as hard as we have tried. For another, what would be the mob's advantage in killing Lester? Someone else would take his place here, and as I see it, his murder would have accomplished nothing."

"A valid point. You mentioned Roland Marchbank a few minutes ago. What is his role here?"

"Roland is assistant executive director. As such, he served as Lester's right-hand man."

"Will he take over the top spot now?"

"That has not yet been decided," she said, spacing her words.

"Who does the deciding?"

"I'm sure you know who Weldon Dunagan is."

"The grocery store magnate."

"Oh, come on, Archie, you know more than that about him, unless I have badly overrated you."

"Okay, you have smoked me out; I will start over. He is the individual who has essentially bankrolled this outfit."

"Bravo, Mr. G.!" She clapped her hands. "Without him, we would be nothing. He has detested the crime syndicate for years, and Three-G is his way of trying to do something about it. He wanted to set us up in luxurious quarters, but Lester felt that would send a bad message to the public, so we have what you see here." She spread her arms. "Actually, these offices are more than adequate, so there's nothing to complain about.

"And before we go any further, Archie, I need to say that although our success in combating the syndicate has been negligible, we *have* done better in other areas, specifically local government. Our investigations have identified graft in some city departments and have led to arrests and indictments. I could get specific if you like."

"Not necessary, and congratulations. Does Mr. Dunagan take an active role here?"

"Not exactly," Laura said. "Oh, on rare occasions, he sits in on one of our meetings, but his attitude essentially is that you hire good people and leave them alone to do their jobs. Even when he does come here, he says very little during our meetings."

"I gather he does not have a high opinion of our fair city's police."

"You gather correctly. And for some reason, he has been particularly critical of Inspector Cramer of Homicide."

"Interesting. Do you have any idea why?"

"I haven't a clue," she said. "But on a couple of occasions when he was here, he made disparaging remarks of a general nature about the inspector. Nothing specific."

Long ago, I learned that when interviewing an individual, it was always best to save the toughest questions for last. That moment had now come.

"How would you describe the morale here when Mr. Pierce was in charge?"

Laura blinked as if surprised. "Well, fine, absolutely fine, why would it be otherwise?"

"Beats me. I'm just a detective trying to detect. Did everyone here get along well with everyone else?"

She seemed to tighten up and paused a beat before responding. "Oh, there were the occasional differences of opinion among us, but nothing that I would term major."

"I gather Mr. Marchbank was considered to be the second in command."

"He definitely *was* the second in command," she snapped.

"So will he replace Lester Pierce as the executive director of Three-G?"

"As I told you before, that has not yet been announced, but I can only assume he will." Laura's tone was decidedly cooler than earlier.

"Do you feel you should get the job?"

"Really, I find that question to be impertinent."

"What is so impertinent about it? You clearly are a talented individual, and I can only assume you have a certain amount of ambition, which is by no means a bad thing." My comment seemed to calm the waters, at least for the moment.

"Of course I do have some goals," she said, shifting in her chair. "Everyone possessed of self-respect does. Do I think I would make a good executive director? Yes, but then, so would Roland."

"Diplomatically put. Did Mr. Pierce ever suggest to you that he would like you to succeed him?"

Now the tension had returned, as I figured it would. "I'm curious as to why you would think Lester should want me to take over in his stead."

"As I understand it, there had been some speculation that he had his eye on the governor's mansion, and if that was the case, he would naturally be planning for Three-G's future."

"That governor business was nothing more than a rumor, at least as far as I know," she said, "probably circulated by one of the newspapers. Lester certainly never mentioned to me any political ambitions he had, or to anyone else here in my presence."

"The press has been known to start rumors, all right, it's one of the things they do best. How would you describe your relationship with Mr. Pierce?" I asked in the most innocent tone I could muster.

Laura glowered at me, and she had one dandy glower. "You have been leading up to that since you walked in here, haven't you?"

"What I have been doing is trying to learn from you as much as possible about the operations and personalities here. I assume you want the killer of Lester Pierce caught as badly as Nero Wolfe and I do."

"I am sure that you know very well—very damned well— that there have been rumors about Lester and me. I had no comment about these rumors when asked about them by the police, and I certainly have no comment about them to you. Now if you will please excuse me, I have given you more than enough of my time, and as you can see, I have a pile of paperwork staring at me."

She turned to some paperwork on her desk, head down. I had been dismissed, much as Weldon Dunagan had dismissed me. At this rate, I could get a complex.

CHAPTER 13

"I failed miserably in my attempt to enrapture the comely Laura Cordwell," I told Wolfe on my return to the brownstone.

He dog-eared a page in his book and set it down. "Report."

I unloaded my verbatim report of our conversation as he sat back, eyes closed. When I had finished, he blinked once and said, "She appears to be in the throes of remorse over her amatory adventures."

"Maybe, but throes or not, and amatory or not, she strikes me as one very smart and very calculating number. Could she have had Pierce dispatched? Possibly, although I will lay odds against it. And before you ask if my opinion is in any way swayed by her beauty—and she is beautiful—the answer is no. As attractive as she is, she did nothing to stimulate my—what do you term it?—amatory senses, and I'm not sure I can tell you why. Anyway, I see this venture as an exercise in failure."

"Not necessarily," Wolfe said. "You surely have learned more about the woman and her motivations than you think. Did you detect any remorse on her part over Mr. Pierce's death?"

"I did not, although she may be one of those people who are able to hide their grief well."

"Perhaps, although I am inclined to subscribe to your description of Miss Cordwell as *calculating*."

"No question about it. Now I suppose you want me to tackle Roland Marchbank, right?"

"That already has been taken care of," Wolfe said dismissively.

"So you're pulling that old stunt again, eh?" Over the years, the man who signs my checks has developed the habit of giving assignments to others without bothering to inform me. He claims he does so because he does not want me to become distracted from other tasks I have been given.

"Let me guess," I went on. "You sent Saul to talk to this Marchbank. He's usually the one you use when you don't feel you can trust me."

"Trust has nothing to do with it," Wolfe replied. "I desired that you give your full concentration to Miss Cordwell."

"Uh-huh. And where, just out of curiosity, did Saul's sit-down with Roland Marchbank take place?"

"At some restaurant in Midtown. I felt it unwise for both of you to be at the Good Government Group's offices simultaneously."

"I presume you plan to debrief Saul privately," I grumped.

"Archie, you are unnecessarily rankled. In fact, I asked Saul to be here tonight at nine to report on his meeting. May I take it you will be present?"

"Sure, why not? I have nothing else to do."

At five to nine, I answered the bell and opened the front door to Saul Panzer.

"So you get the beauty and I get the beast," he said, taking off his brown flat cap and flipping it six feet across the hall to the coatrack, where it hung cleanly. To repeat myself, he almost never misses.

"You know more about my day than I know about yours," I told him. "Let us compare notes."

In the office, Saul settled into the red leather chair after having mixed himself a scotch and soda from the bar cart against the wall. I had a scotch of my own, and Wolfe drank beer.

"Tell us about Mr. Marchbank," Wolfe said.

Saul made a face. "For starters, this character hardly qualifies as Mr. Personality. The biography I read in advance says that he's forty-three, but he looks at least five years older. He is short, which is no sin—so am I—and his puss seems to be fixed in a permanent scowl. He resented what he seemed to feel was an inquisition on my part, although I felt I was the essence of diplomacy and tact.

"'I don't know why I should even bother talking to you,' he said as an opening salvo. 'The police haven't gotten anywhere, why should a bunch of private gumshoes have any better success? And by the way, who hired your boss Wolfe?'

"I told him I had no idea as to the client's identity, that I was only a small cog in the operation. That seemed somehow to please him. I, of course, asked him up front if he had any thoughts about who killed Pierce, and he replied with a sneer: 'The easy answer is the mob, which is probably what you expected me to say, but I am not so sure.'

"When I asked him why he had doubts, he said the crime syndicate had little to gain from the killing, that Three-G would push on, presumably with him at the helm. So I pressed him for other possible murderers, and he just threw up his hands. 'Beats me,' he said. 'If Lester had enemies, I can't imagine who they would be.'

"I then asked how the folks at the Good Government Group got along with one another. 'Quite well,' he said. 'What did you expect? Are you trying to suggest that one of us might have wanted him dead?'

"I told him I just wanted to get a sense of the mood in the office and asked if he, Marchbank, expected to be named executive director.

"'And just why wouldn't I?' he said tartly, looking at me as though I were a simpleton. 'I was the number-two person in the operation, although I sure as hell would never have wanted to get the top job in this way.'

"I then asked if Miss Cordwell might be in the running to head the organization. His answer: 'Laura? Hardly. Oh, she's bright, no question about that. But she still really is far too inexperienced to run things.'

"When I asked Marchbank how the young woman got along with Lester Pierce, he shrugged. 'You will have to ask her that yourself, Mr. Panzer. I don't want to be accused of spreading stories, if you get my drift.'

"I said I didn't get his drift and he laughed, but it wasn't mirthful laughter, more like a cackle. My next question was about Weldon Dunagan and what it was like having him finance Three-G.

"His response was delivered yet again with a sneer, which must be his default expression. He said, 'The guy is so rich that what he gives us must just come out of his petty cash drawer, and it probably gives him a tax deduction to boot. But what the hell, it pays all our salaries and our operating expenses as well, so I'd be a sap to complain, wouldn't I?'"

Wolfe finished his beer and set the glass down. "Did Mr. Marchbank say anything further when you asked if he thought he would be named as the organization's executive director?"

"Yes, he did, and I apologize for not mentioning it."

"You have nothing to apologize for," Wolfe said. "Continue."

"Marchbank added this: 'I am committed to Three-G, whether or not I end up running it. Have you got that?'

"I told him I did, but from his huffy reaction, it seemed to be a case of one who doth protest too much, methinks."

"*Hamlet*, Act III, Scene 2," Wolfe said, dipping his chin in salute to Saul's knowledge of Shakespeare. "Overall, Mr. Marchbank seems not to be a happy individual," he continued. "Would you concur?"

"Totally," Saul said. "I am not sure the guy likes anybody, and—" He was interrupted by the phone, which I answered simply "Archie Goodwin" because it was after business hours.

"I thought you'd want to know about this," Lon Cohen said. "We just got word that Cramer has been put on permanent leave, which is one step from forced retirement. The morning papers will beat us on this, but we're still planning a page-one piece summarizing the inspector's long career."

"What about Rowcliff?" I asked, causing both Wolfe and Saul to raise their eyebrows, since they were only getting my end of the conversation.

"Still acting head of Homicide, so we're told by that mealy-mouthed hack who spits out press releases for the department. I've gotta believe Rowcliff is licking his chops because the top spot is now so close he can taste it."

"Anything else?"

"Nope, that's it for now," Lon said. "While we are on the line, anything that you would like to tell me?"

"Just that you are one lucky so-and-so at the poker table."

I got a laugh. "Don't tell me that you're still sore about that full house of mine that beat your three of a kind?"

"No comment. See you next Thursday night," I said, signing off. I swiveled to face Wolfe and Saul to fill them in on Lon's end of the conversation. Wolfe scowled and Saul slapped a palm against his forehead. "The very idea of Rowcliff heading up Homicide—or any other operation for that matter—is simply too dreadful to contemplate," he said, shaking his head in disbelief.

"I share your repugnance," Wolfe said. "The current commissioner, who is manifestly a lackwit, has been looking for ways to get rid of Mr. Cramer for some time, in large measure because he is the lone department head who is a holdover from the previous administration. The lack of progress in the Pierce murder only serves to strengthen Mr. O'Hara's hand."

"Yeah, although O'Hara pulled Cramer off the case before he had any chance to get started," I argued.

"True enough, but with the outcry about the killing that came from the newspapers, the civic groups, and the public, it became relatively easy for the commissioner to act in a way that appeared to be decisive, whatever its motivation."

"Making Cramer a sacrificial lamb," Saul observed.

"Some lamb!" I said. "If anything, I would call him a sacrificial lion. There has never been anything the least bit lamblike about our dear old inspector."

That drew a chuckle from Saul and the hint of a smile from Wolfe. "Enough silliness, where do we go from here?" I asked.

"I am open to suggestions, gentlemen," Wolfe replied.

On rare occasions over the years, my boss has delivered that "I am open to suggestions" line, and usually for one of two reasons: Either he's reached a dead end or he has lost interest. This time, I think it was the latter. He started out having little enthusiasm for the case, but briefly stirred himself to action because of Saul's mugging. Now he seemed to have reverted to his original ho-hum attitude.

I was about to cut loose with a sarcastic comment when Saul piped up. "I think we need to dig more deeply into Lester Pierce's history," he said.

"Go on," Wolfe replied with what I felt was at least a spark of interest.

"For instance, I recall that the man had several offspring."

"Three, two sons and a daughter, according to Lily Rowan and to the articles about Pierce's shooting," I said.

"Do you know anything about them?" Saul pressed. "Their ages, where they reside, what they do for a living, how they got along with their parents?"

Wolfe turned to me. "Do you have answers?"

"No, sir."

"Very well. Your point is well taken, Saul. Archie will learn their whereabouts and interview each of them."

"What if one or more of the younger Pierces lives out of town?" I asked.

"We shall ford that stream when we come to it. Now, if you both will excuse me, I am retiring," Wolfe said, rising and walking out of the office in the direction of the elevator.

"So it appears I have my assignment," I told Saul. "I've got to find out where the Pierce siblings are located. I could call Lon Cohen, but that would only start him asking more questions, and I would prefer to get the information some other way."

"Let me see what I can learn, Archie," Saul said. "I can probably get you what you need."

"I know you've got plenty of sources, but just be aware that if one or more of the Pierce offspring happens to live somewhere well outside the environs of New York City, you will almost surely be the one to make the trip. You know how Wolfe feels about losing my services for more than a day."

"I just hope I don't have to hop a plane and go off to the ends of the continent or beyond. I've just gotten myself a new assignment from a jeweler who claims one of his six employees is dipping into the till, and he wants fast work."

"I await the results of your research," I told him, going over to the bar cart against the wall and refilling our scotches. "How about some gin rummy before you head off into the night?"

"You will be sorry," Saul said.

CHAPTER 14

It turned out to be bad news and then good news for Saul. The bad news was that I beat him at gin rummy to the tune of nine dollars, a relative rarity for me. The good news was that he would not have to board an airplane. All three of the Pierce offspring lived in the New York area, so they became my babies, so to speak.

"Okay, here's the situation, Archie," Saul reported on the phone the next morning. "Malcolm Pierce—he is the eldest at thirty-three—works at one of the big investment banks on Wall Street, is married with no children, and lives at the Dakota. His wife, Annette, is co-owner of a chichi boutique up on Fifth Avenue, close to the Metropolitan Museum."

"We're talking big bucks," I remarked, knowing a little about the cost of living in that historic old building on the Upper West Side.

"I don't have the impression money is a major concern in the Pierce family," Saul said. "The middle sibling, Marianne, is thirty-one, single, and apparently something of a looker. She has a place down in the Village. She's an editor with one of the big women's fashion magazines, *Today's Styles*, so that means she works in the heart of Midtown.

"The youngest of the three, Mark, is twenty-nine and toils as an art director at the Masters and Price advertising agency on Madison Avenue, where he's something of a *wunderkind*, so I'm told. He's married, commutes by train into the city from their home in Dobbs Ferry up on the Hudson, and has one child, a toddler. His wife, Pamela, is a freelance writer whose office is at home."

"Hmm, must be something about the letter 'M' that the elder Pierces were partial to when they named their children."

"So it would seem," Saul said. He proceeded to give me work and home telephone numbers for the trio of Pierces.

"Put me down as impressed," I told him. "Where did you get that pile of information so quickly?"

"It is all in who you know, my son," he replied, "and I just happen to know a certain someone on the society pages of a certain major New York newspaper—not the *Gazette*, by the way. Both she and her publication must remain nameless."

"Of course they must. Now you are free to find out just which of his staff is robbing your jeweler client."

"I already have a pretty good idea, but I've got to get clicking, because my man is a nervous Nellie, and I'm afraid he's going to have a heart attack or a stroke if I don't quickly nail the culprit."

"*Culprit*, is it? Now you're using words like the world-weary, hard-bitten New York operative I've always known you to be."

"Aw, shucks, I'm just a country boy adjusting to the ways of the big city."

"Country boy, eh? Somehow I've never thought of Brooklyn as part of rural America."

"Just goes to show how little you know. Now I am off to the rarified world of diamonds and rubies and emeralds while you rub shoulders with members of one of New York's most well-known and well-heeled families."

For no particular reason, I decided to start my Pierce clan interviews with Malcolm, the eldest sibling. I dialed the number Saul had given to me at the investment bank, and to my surprise, Malcolm himself answered on the first ring. I decided on the direct approach.

"Hello, Mr. Pierce, my name is Archie Goodwin, from Nero Wolfe's office, and I would like to talk to you about your father's death."

"I don't know you, Mr. Goodwin," Malcolm said in an amiable tone, "although I most certainly have heard of Nero Wolfe. How does he happen to be interested in . . . in what happened to my father?"

"Mr. Wolfe has been engaged to learn who was responsible for the killing."

"Really? Who is paying your boss?" Pierce said, sounding surprised.

"The person who hired Mr. Wolfe chooses not to be identified at this time."

"Well, the police surely haven't gotten very far, have they? Maybe that's because they realize that it's fruitless to try tackling the Mafia. Have you spoken to my mother? You really should."

"No, not yet. We felt it was too soon for that," I improvised.

"Mm. Do you want to discuss this with me on the telephone?"

"I would prefer it to be in person, if you don't mind."

"I do not mind one bit, Mr. Goodwin, although I would rather not have any conversation take place in my office. It tends not to be a very private setting."

"I understand."

"Let me suggest that you come to our home in the Dakota. I trust you know where that is," he said with a self-deprecating chuckle.

"Everybody knows where the Dakota is," I said with a chuckle of my own. "When is convenient for you?"

"Actually, I happen to have a very light workload today and I was thinking of leaving the office early. What about three o'clock this afternoon?"

I told him that would be fine with me. When Wolfe came down from the plant rooms at eleven, I filled him in and he nodded, turning to the mail I had stacked neatly on his desk blotter.

"Any instructions?"

"Nothing specific. I trust you will ferret out any information you deem useful."

After lunch I flagged a yellow cab on Eighth Avenue and rode north on the artery as it changed its name to Central Park West. The taxi dropped me at Seventy-Second Street, where I hopped out and gazed up at one of the city's most identifiable structures. The Dakota is not tall by Manhattan standards, around ten stories at the outside, but it looms large in its setting like some grand castle plucked from another era, with curved bay windows, dormers, balconies, ironwork, gingerbread touches, and a multigabled roof. I had never set foot in the building, although Lily Rowan told me about a soiree she had once attended in a lavish apartment with a guest list including a famous opera diva, three ambassadors, a former American president, and two Pulitzer Prize–winning authors.

I adjusted my tie and nodded to a ramrod-straight doorman who wore a peaked cap and a long coat, both of which boldly bore the words *The Dakota* in letters easy to read from a distance. After someone determined that I was expected at the Malcolm Pierce residence, I rode up in an elevator to the sixth floor. As the operator watched from his car, I pressed the buzzer and was admitted to the apartment by a perky maid wearing a crisp gray uniform and a lacy cap like someone out of a 1940s movie.

I found myself in a vaulted, circular foyer with a multicolored marble floor and a ten-foot coffered ceiling. This round room was big enough to accommodate a six-piece dance band fronted by a girl singer. As I took in the scene, a voice said, "Quite a space, isn't it, Mr. Goodwin?"

Malcolm Pierce had stepped in without a sound. Tall, sandy-haired, and clad in brown slacks, a camel hair sport coat, and an open-collared shirt, he looked like he had just stepped out of a full-page advertisement in a men's fashion magazine.

"I was just admiring the setup," I responded. "I have never been in the Dakota before."

"It is a marvelous place, dates back to the 1880s," he said. "They sure don't build 'em like this anymore. Let's talk in the library."

"First, Mr. Wolfe and I want to extend our condolences about your loss."

"That is very kind of you, Mr. Goodwin," Malcolm Pierce said. If he was still grieving, he held it in well.

I followed my host down a long hall that made me think the apartment went on forever. We entered a dark-paneled room with floor-to-ceiling bookcases, an elaborate chandelier, and a fireplace with a painting above it that looked to be a Matisse, and almost surely was an original. My host gestured me to an easy chair while he nodded toward a bar in one corner. "Can I get you anything to drink?"

"A bit early in the day for me, thanks anyway."

"It is for me, too, Mr. Goodwin, but I always like to ask," he said, taking a chair opposite mine. "Now, tell me how I can be of help in this sad business."

"To be honest, I am not sure you can, but we—that is, Nero Wolfe and I—are talking to as many people as we can in the hopes that we'll learn more about your father's death."

He nodded. No question, Malcolm Pierce was one clean-cut specimen, with razor-cut hair, blue eyes, straight nose, and square jaw, looks he inherited from his father, whose photo I had seen in the newspapers. "I don't suppose you are going to tell me who your client is, are you?"

"No, as I said on the telephone, that individual has chosen to remain anonymous."

Another nod. "Have you spoken to my brother or sister?"

"No, but I plan to."

"And to repeat what I said on the phone, you really also should talk to my mother, that's important."

"I'm sure we will. Do you have any thoughts as to who would want to kill your father?"

"I certainly do not mean to sound rude or dismissive, Mr. Goodwin, but it seems glaringly obvious to me that the crime syndicate was behind what happened, as I also said to that police-man, I believe Rowcliff was his name. I know it is extremely difficult to pin anything on the mob and make it stick, but it is hard to come to any other conclusion.

"As you and your boss know, my father had fought against organized crime for years, and it seems clear they finally got tired of his attacks on them. Other than the mob, he had no enemies that I was ever aware of. My guess is that my brother and sister will tell you the same thing."

"What about your father's personal life?" I asked, knowing the question might get me tossed off the premises.

"I really don't know anything about that, Mr. Goodwin," he said without the slightest hint of animosity or resentment, although he stiffened slightly. "That would be a question for my mother, although I honestly can't tell you what her reaction would be."

"Was it your impression that your father was happy with the staff he worked with at the Good Government Group?"

"I believe so, although we did not talk a lot about it. I won't say he was exactly secretive about his work, but he tended to compartmentalize the various areas of his life, and he rarely talked to me about the goings-on at the Good Government Group."

"Other than your siblings or your mother, is there anyone you can think of who might be helpful in our investigation?"

He laughed. "Why not try the head of the syndicate, what's his name—Ralph Mars? Although I doubt you'll have much luck getting him to open up. Nobody else ever has, as far as I know."

"Do you have any reason to doubt that the mob was behind your father's killing?"

"Absolutely none whatever," Malcolm said. "To me, it's your classic open-and-shut case. I believe the police aren't pursuing my father's murder more vigorously because they know the syndicate never gets nailed. Those people can kill with impunity."

"It seems I have taken enough of your time," I said, looking at my watch and standing.

"Not at all, Mr. Goodwin. I am just happy that you are concerned about what happened to my father, regardless of who your client is. Does your Nero Wolfe have any reason to doubt it was a mob-driven murder?"

"I believe Mr. Wolfe is open to numerous options. He does not always share his mental processes with me."

"It must be interesting working for him, though, based on what I have read about him in the newspapers over the years."

"Oh, it is, and frustrating at times, too. But then, he is a genius and I am merely a spear carrier."

"I doubt that very much, Mr. Goodwin," Malcolm Pierce said, flashing a grin. "And to repeat myself, make sure someone—you or Mr. Wolfe perhaps—talks to my mother. I believe she will be up to it and may be of some help in discussing my father. She is a strong woman."

I thanked him for his time and for the opportunity to see the legendary Dakota, which brought yet another grin from the eldest of the Piece siblings.

By the time I got back to the brownstone, Wolfe was seated in the office with beer and a book after his visit with the orchids on the roof. As I walked in, he looked up, his expression questioning.

"Malcolm Pierce is without doubt smooth and amiable," I said.

"Are you using smooth as a synonym for evasive or perhaps duplicitous?"

"Not necessarily. It is just that he always seemed quick to respond, with no hemming and hawing, no indecision whatever. He seems absolutely convinced the Mafia was behind his father's killing."

I then proceeded to give him a verbatim report of our conversation. When I had finished, Wolfe went back to his book without comment.

"Do you feel I asked all the right questions?"

"It was an adequate interview. When will you talk to the others?"

"I thought I would make calls this afternoon and try to see both of them tomorrow."

Wolfe returned to his book, which I took to be an unspoken "satisfactory." I did in fact call both Marianne and Mark Pierce and got less than enthusiastic responses from each.

"What could be accomplished by my seeing you?" the Pierce daughter said when I reached her at her magazine office on Seventh Avenue, identified myself, and offered my sympathy.

"I have told the police everything I know, which isn't very damned much. I don't see how Nero Wolfe, who I know claims to be a genius, can make a rabbit jump out of a hat, so to speak."

I explained to Marianne that she had nothing to lose by seeing me, and that maybe, just maybe, she might have something to say that, without her realizing, might help with our investigation.

"I doubt that very much, Mr. Goodwin," she responded. "Besides, I happen to be extremely busy at work. I have what you might call a high-pressure job."

"Then perhaps you could benefit from an after-hours drink tomorrow to relieve some of that pressure. On me, of course."

After a pause of several seconds, followed by a sigh, she said, "You are one persistent cuss, aren't you?"

"So I have been told. And some people have even dared to call me personable, as well as affable."

I detected an ever-so-slight snicker at the other end of the line. "All right, Mr. Goodwin, do you know where my office is?"

"I do, and I also recall that there's a quiet little bar just across the street with a great jazz pianist, whose name, if I recall, is Herbie."

"I know the place, too, very well in fact, and it is Herbie; what about six thirty tomorrow?"

"That sounds fine. How will I know you, Miss Pierce?"

"You can start by calling me Marianne. I'll be wearing . . . let's see . . . a gray turtleneck sweater and a gray skirt. And just how will I recognize you?"

"I'll probably be wearing a smirk and a blue blazer."

"With brass buttons on it?"

"Absolutely not. I definitely am not the collegiate type. See you at six thirty tomorrow."

The next call was to Mark Pierce at his advertising agency on Madison Avenue. My luck held when he answered his own phone. As with his siblings, I expressed my condolences and said I wanted to see him regarding our investigation into his father's death.

"I mean no disrespect, Mr. Goodwin, but I really can see no reason to talk to you," he said after I had introduced myself. "There is nothing whatever I can add to what I already have told the police."

"Speaking of the police, are you happy with how they have performed in all of this?"

"Hah! I'm sure that you can answer that one yourself," Pierce growled.

"Then what do you have to lose by seeing me?"

"At the risk of sounding like someone who is indispensable, what I have to lose is time, which for me is a valuable commodity."

"When I talk to people, I try to be as efficient as possible. I do not want to waste your time any more than you want to have it wasted."

He replied after a pause of several seconds. "All right, Mr. . . . Goodwin, is it? As it happens, I am going to be working from home tomorrow, as I do about once a week. I live up in Dobbs Ferry. Do you know where that is?"

"I do, passed through there a couple of times. It seems like a nice, peaceful village."

"It is that, and just far enough from the city so that I feel I'm in another world. I don't know if you've got a car or would take the train, but if you can be at my home around eleven forty-five tomorrow morning, I will take a break from work and give you a half hour or so, but not much more."

"A half hour should be fine, and I will be driving up," I said, and I took down his address and directions. I would be missing both lunch and dinner in the brownstone. Fritz would not like that, but then, I was hardly wild about it myself.

CHAPTER 15

The drive north the next morning was surprisingly pleasant for mid-November, and when I am behind the wheel, no matter the destination, I always find myself in a positive frame of mind. Traffic was light as I took the Henry Hudson Parkway north, and at some point around Yonkers, the road became the Saw Mill River Parkway. After I had passed through Hastings-on-Hudson, I saw a welcoming sign announcing that I was entering Dobbs Ferry.

Following the directions I had been given by Mark Pierce, I had no trouble finding my destination, a two-story gray-and-white frame house with a wraparound porch on a quiet street well away from the town's business district. My guess is it was built sometime late in the nineteenth century. In response to my pushing a buzzer, the front door was pulled open by a slender, red-haired woman whose smile made me feel welcome.

"You are Mr. Goodwin, right?" I pleaded guilty.

"I'm Pamela, Mark's wife. He's just finishing up some work. Can I get you coffee?"

"Yes, I would like some," I said as she led me through the front hall and into the cheerful, yellow-walled living room, whose large front windows looked out on a park that sloped down to the gray waters of the Hudson two blocks distant.

"You have got a terrific view here," I told Pamela as she set a hot cup of java on an end table next to the sofa where I had parked myself.

"Yes, we love it," she said. "That's a big part of what sold us on the house. There is something very soothing about watching a great river move slowly by on its way to the city and the sea. What a history this old valley has!"

I was about to respond when a stocky, black-haired man soundlessly stepped into the room. Mark Pierce could not have looked less like his brother, Malcolm. "Mr. Goodwin, I see you have met my wife," he said with a slight grin as we shook hands. "I hope Pamela has kept you entertained. She has the personality in our family. I'm afraid I am the somber—some would say dour—half of the team."

"Nonsense!" she told her husband. "You are artistic, thoughtful, and introspective, while I tend to run off at the mouth and be something of a dreamer."

"We can discuss our personality traits later and not bore Mr. Goodwin with them," Pierce said with pursed lips. "He and I are going to talk up in my office."

Carrying my cup of coffee with me, I followed him upstairs to a room that also had a view of the Hudson. It clearly was a working space, dominated by a slanted drawing board covered with sheets of paper that had sketches on them. Other sketches were tacked to a corkboard.

"Pardon this mess," my host said. "I'm in the middle of a campaign for a brand of coffee that our agency just landed. In fact, it happens to be the brand that you're drinking right now. At the agency, we always use the products we advertise. I'm usually at the office about four days a week, but it can be such a madhouse that I find when I'm under a deadline, I can usually get more done here."

"I promised that I would not take a lot of your time, and I will keep that promise," I told him.

"Good. As I was coming downstairs, I overheard Pamela tell you that we bought this house because of its location. That's partially true, but we also liked the size of the place. It has given us the room for two separate work spaces: my studio and her office right next door. She's a freelance magazine writer and a good one, if I do say so myself.

"She's always got assignments. And the walls are so thick that we can't hear each other, not that we make all that much noise. But it does give us each a sense of privacy."

"Have you lived here long?"

"Three years now. We were in the city before, in Hell's Kitchen on the West Side, and we moved here when Pamela was pregnant. Our little guy, Timmy, is napping down the hall in the nursery, which is connected to our master bedroom."

"Nice layout all around. Did you grow up in Manhattan?"

"I did. My parents had a co-op on the Upper East Side. I lived there until I went off to a design school in Rhode Island."

"Did you have what you would call a happy childhood?" I asked as we sat in two beanbag chairs in one corner of the spacious room.

"Mr. Goodwin, I cannot believe that you drove all the way up here to talk about my formative years, so to speak. I thought that you and that so-called genius boss of yours were concerned with my father's murder."

"We are, but we felt maybe there was something in the past that might explain what has happened."

"I can't imagine what that would be. It seems to me that Nero Wolfe and the police either don't think the mob is behind my father's death or they simply do not know how to tackle those goons," Mark said with a scowl. "I have to question myself whether the thugs are behind Dad's killing."

"And why is that?"

"Well, look," he said, spreading his arms, "what does the syndicate have to gain by this murder? Nothing, absolutely nothing! The Good Government Group already has shown, I am sorry to say, that it has no ability whatever to rein in the mob's operations in the city. So why would they try to rile up the cops with such a senseless killing? It seems like they would be creating an unnecessary headache for themselves."

"Let sleeping dogs lie, is that it?" I said.

"Exactly! And it seems to me that Three-G is something like a sleeping dog. Let's face it; they are no real threat to the mobsters, whatever my father may have liked to believe. Although I have to say in defense of the organization, it *has* been more successful in its investigations into some of the city's departments. But still, Three-G's main thrust has always been to the crime syndicate. I refuse to believe they killed my father."

"Maybe that's why Nero Wolfe is looking into other options."

"And just what might some other options be?" Mark said.

"We're not entirely sure. Other than the crime syndicate, did your father have any enemies you are aware of?"

"Not at all, as I told the police," he said, looking none too subtly at his wristwatch. "People seemed drawn to him, to the degree that he was being encouraged to run for governor, as you may be aware."

"Yes, I had read about that. Is there any likelihood your father had a secret of some sort that might have endangered him?"

"Of course it's possible, Mr. Goodwin. For heaven's sake, everyone has secrets, and most of us go to great lengths to ensure they remain that way. If he had any secrets, I am afraid that I'm not aware of them."

"Do you think his supposed interest in running for governor would have somehow endangered him?"

"I simply can't see his political ambitions causing anyone to want to kill him."

"Would you say he and your mother had a good marriage?"

"As good as most, I suppose," Mark said. "If they ever fought, I never heard about it, although you should ask my brother and sister. I'm sure you plan to question them, if you have not already. Now, I'm sorry to be so brief, but if you will excuse me, I am in the middle of that campaign I mentioned earlier to make a certain coffee 'the breakfast choice from Maine to California and everywhere in between.'"

Mark Pierce stood, which I saw as my cue that the interview had come to an end, and he pointedly turned his back on me, going over to his drawing board, sitting and peering at one of his sketches of a man grinning at the cup of coffee he held in both hands as if it were a prized possession. I got up, no longer a welcome guest. If indeed I ever had been one, at least by the man of the house.

When I got to the bottom of the stairway, Pamela materialized. "Done already?" she asked, smiling.

"Yes, and I appreciate your husband's time and your hospitality," I told her. "And the coffee was delicious. You have a fine home. I hope you continue to enjoy it for years to come."

"Thank you so much, Mr. Goodwin. We have been very happy here. I am only sorry for what happened to Mark's father. He was a true gentleman. I do so hope the person who planned his murder is found."

"So do I, Mrs. Pierce," I said as I stepped out of the house.

Driving back to New York, I reviewed my impression of Mark Pierce. Surly might be too strong a descriptive, but Wolfe, whose vocabulary is far larger than mine, probably could come up with a better word. One thing seemed certain: The younger Pierce son did not seem overly broken up over his father's violent death. But then, people react to tragedy in far different ways from one another. I know that when my own father died, I was devastated internally but showed very little outward effect, to the point that an aunt remarked, "Archie seems very cold about all of this."

I had to wonder if Mark knew about his father's amorous activities. If Lily Rowan and her friends were aware of these escapades, it seems likely that his offspring all would have realized what was going on as well. Assuming they did know, it is certainly understandable they would choose not to acknowledge the transgressions. In times of crisis, most families tend to present a united front against the outside.

I stopped in Yonkers at a diner I had patronized before and ordered what I considered to be their special, a corned beef on rye sandwich, along with a glass of milk and a slice of apple pie. "Your corned beef is as good as ever," I told a waitress who had been there for years.

"I remember you," she said, grinning. "I've got a great memory. I never forget a face, and besides, this isn't the first time you've commented on the sandwich. I'll send your compliments to Lou back in the kitchen. He likes to get good reviews for his work."

I had stopped at the diner for two reasons: I was hungry, and when I miss a meal in the brownstone, Wolfe invariably asks on my return, "Have you eaten?"

I garaged the car at Curran's, and when I got home, Wolfe was sitting at his desk in the office working last Sunday's *New York Times* crossword puzzle. I waited until he had filled the very last square—he never likes to be interrupted—and then reported on the Dobbs Ferry expedition.

When I had finished my recitation, Wolfe took a drink of after-lunch coffee and carefully set his cup down. "From your report, young Mr. Pierce sounds somewhat morose." Ah, there—he had found a better adjective!

"Morose or otherwise, he certainly did not have much to contribute about his father."

"You are to see his sister this evening?"

"For drinks. Do you think I should vary the line of questioning?"

"Not necessarily, although you may want to mount a frontal attack and ask Miss Pierce if she had knowledge of her father's liaisons," Wolfe said. "But it would be advisable to pose this well after you have spent some time with the young woman. If you were to broach the subject at the beginning of the evening, she might very well bolt, and you would be left with nothing but an empty chair at a table for two."

Wolfe was right, of course, although he did not have to stress to me the importance of asking the tough questions late in a conversation. Such was the lesson our newspaper friend Lon Cohen of the *Gazette* had drilled into me years ago, and as you will recall, I had also used this "tough question last" approach earlier with Laura Cordwell.

"Archie, in any interview, particularly with someone who's got something to hide, you must start slowly," Lon had said.

"That is what I tell all our young reporters. Throw out some easy questions at the beginning to relax the subject, loosen him or her up.

"Then gradually, very gradually, start getting tougher with what you're asking. The worst thing that can happen is that whomever you're grilling tells you to go to hell and walks away. And by then, maybe you will have already learned a lot and gotten some good quotes. But just don't blow an interview from the very start. That has happened more than once here, I am sorry to say. Overeager reporters have cost the paper many a good story."

CHAPTER 16

With Saul's words of wisdom in mind, I set off on foot that evening for the bar that sat directly across Seventh Avenue from the towering magazine company building where Marianne Pierce toiled. I'd been in the place a few times over the years at cocktail time and invariably found it to be pleasantly low-key, particularly with its jazz pianist, who I now know was indeed named Herbie. Today was no exception.

I rotated the revolving door into the darkened space at precisely six thirty and was greeted with the pleasant sounds of the piano over the murmur of multiple conversations. From out of the room's dimness, an attractive woman with shoulder-length blond hair emerged and came toward me. She wore a gray turtleneck sweater and matching skirt.

"The smirk gave you away all right," Marianne Pierce said, head cocked and with hands on hips.

"Darn, and here I've always thought the blue blazer was my true signature look," I replied.

"That, too, and very natty, I must say. Shall we find a booth, or are you the barstool type?"

"I've done both, although I prefer a booth, it's more intimate."

"Ah, so we are going to be intimate, is that it?"

"All right, let me rephrase it. A booth is more conversation friendly. How's that?"

"You're a glib one, aren't you? A booth it is."

We settled in toward the back and ordered drinks, a vodka martini for her and a scotch on the rocks for me. They were delivered quickly by a waitress who seemed to know Marianne.

"So, Archie Goodwin, private eye, I want to know exactly what it's like working for the great Nero Wolfe," she said after sampling her drink, nodding, and licking her lips.

"Where to start? The man is many things—irascible, eccentric, inscrutable, immovable, impassive, phlegmatic, and—oh yes—a genius."

"You sound like you're reading from Mr. Roget's *Thesaurus*," she said. "I will try to act impressed."

"Don't bother. Those probably are all words I have learned from Nero Wolfe over the years. He has quite the vocabulary."

"Is the man difficult to work for?"

"Sometimes. He rarely leaves home, but he does not hesitate to send me out on a whim, and he never puts off until tomorrow what I can do today."

"Poor baby," Marianne said, laughing. "You sound as if you are very put-upon."

"Not really. I have few complaints."

"That's good. I am puzzled about something: Why is it that Nero Wolfe is investigating my father's murder? Who hired him? And what makes him think, as I do, that the crime syndicate was *not* behind what happened?"

"First, our client chooses to remain anonymous, and second, an individual Mr. Wolfe and I highly esteem was beaten up because he got curious about your father's death and started making inquiries. That got my boss extremely angry, and some details of our friend's beating made it seem that perhaps the mob may not have been behind the killing of your father."

"So Nero Wolfe is taking on this case out of the goodness of his heart, is that what you are telling me?"

"I would not go that far. He does very few things out of the goodness of his heart, to use your term. But he is fiercely protective of the very few people he calls his friends, and he also is critical of those who he feels jump to quick conclusions."

"Like perhaps anyone who immediately assumes the crime syndicate was behind my father's murder?"

"Yes, that's a good example. Do you have any thoughts as to why he was gunned down?"

Marianne studied her half-consumed martini, perhaps lost in thought. "I happen to agree with your boss," she said. "It would be simple to pass off this shooting as just another mob hit, which is the easy way out, particularly for the police. But that just does not make a lot of sense to me."

"Go on."

"Well, look, as much as I loved my father, and I did and I miss him very much, he and his small and dedicated band really were not ever much of a threat to organized crime. Oh, they got the newspapers to write editorials and do in-depth reports on the Mafia all right, but where did it get them? What did they accomplish? Nothing, really. That being the case, it seems to me that the best thing Ralph Mars and his boys could do was to leave well enough alone."

"Perhaps you have a point," I said as I lit cigarettes for both of us with my Zippo. "If what you are saying is true, it means your father must have had at least one other enemy."

"I suppose we all make a certain number of enemies throughout our lives, maybe some of them inadvertently or unconsciously," Marianne said. "I am sure I have, and you probably have as well."

"I won't deny that. Let us both for the moment agree that the mob did *not* kill your father. Can you think of any other candidates, anyone at all?"

"The police asked me that question, and I told them I could not conceive of someone else who would have had that much hatred for him."

"From what I have read and heard, he must have been extremely well respected," I said, ordering another round of drinks.

Marianne smiled ruefully. "He was, Archie. As you may be aware, a movement was under way to get Daddy to run for governor, which says a lot."

"It does, all right. Do you think he would have dropped Three-G for a chance to run the Empire State?"

"I really don't know. He and I never talked about it, although once at a family dinner, he said something like, 'If they ever put me in charge up in Albany, you are going to see a lot of rats leave the creaky ship that is referred to as the SS *New York State*.'"

"Can you think of something that might have prevented your father from running for governor?"

"The entrenched interests, I suppose. He would have been a threat to a lot of old-line politicians who have run the state forever."

"Anything in your father's past that would have been a liability?"

She fixed me with a look that was less than friendly. "Just what are you trying to say?"

"I'm not sure."

"Oh, I think you are, Archie. Let us not get cute here. You took your good old time to bring this up, so we should get things out on the table right now. And don't play the innocent with me; it won't wash."

"I will ask the question again," I said evenly. "Is there anything in your father's past that would be a liability?"

"May I assume you have talked to one or the other of my brothers?"

"I have seen both of them."

"And what have they told you about my father's private life?"

"Nothing whatever, and I will take an oath to that effect if you want me to, assuming we can find a Bible in this den of depravity."

She sniffed. "For some reason, I believe you. My brothers, they can be incredibly naive, or else they just close their eyes to the world around them. Mal, bless him, has always been something of a mama's boy. To him, our mother could never do anything wrong. Maybe it's something about him being the eldest child. And Mark, well, he is a driven creative type who lives to develop the next great advertising campaign, and the rest of the world be damned."

"I am not sure what that proves."

"There you go again, trying to play the innocent. Archie, I've been around the block a few times. Three men have proposed to me, and I've turned them all down."

"Their loss."

"And my gain. I did not bring that up to pat myself on the back. Now, dammit, ask the question you are dying to ask. Go ahead."

"All right then, what do you know about your father's private life?"

"See, that wasn't so hard to do now, was it? My father was drawn to women, and they were drawn to him. Some of his, shall we say . . . relationships, were not very well-kept secrets, I'm afraid."

"Including with Laura Cordwell?"

She sighed. "Including with Laura, yes."

"I have no idea how many women your father was involved with, but might one of them or one of their friends, relatives, or colleagues have planned his killing?"

"You have a typical man's inflated idea of how strongly a woman is affected by rejection," Marianne told me. "I mentioned that three men had proposed to me—true. But another man dumped me, there's no sugarcoating that. Did I respond by ordering his killing? No, I realized how lucky I was to have avoided what would have been an unhappy relationship."

"I was not necessarily suggesting a woman was behind your father's murder, at least not directly," I replied. "One or another of those women your father was involved with may very well have had either a husband or a fiancé or a relative who wanted to exact revenge."

"Maybe having been a private detective for so long has given you a flair for the dramatic," Marianne said as she ground out her cigarette in an ashtray. "Your scenario seems awfully far-fetched to me."

"No more far-fetched than a lot of other situations we've come across."

"That may be, but I still don't think much of your theory. Changing the subject, what was your impression of my brothers now that I've told you my analysis of them? I'm just curious."

"They both seem to be quite serious minded, based on our relatively brief meetings."

Marianne laughed. "That's one way of putting it. Mark is far more than serious. I'd call him verging on the melancholy."

"Now *you* are using the thesaurus," I joked.

"Well, I do have a decent vocabulary if I do say so," she retorted. "After all, I am an editor. What did you think of Mal?"

"Seems a decent sort, and I gather quite successful, but then all three of you appear to have made a mark in your respective fields."

"That's so, but then we each had a lot of advantages growing up—the best schools, foreign vacations, internships set up by our father—so we should have done well. Back to Mal, as I said he was a mama's boy and in many ways still is. But then, maybe that is to be expected of a firstborn. He has always seen himself as her protector."

"How would you describe your parents' marriage?"

"They seemed to have lived in separate worlds, particularly in the last few years. My mother always immersed herself in good works for all kinds of charities. It seemed like she was forever hosting a luncheon or a fund drive. Daddy had his own charities and passions, most notably, of course, the Good Government Group. He hated the crime syndicate and was determined to put it out of business."

"But it appears that he also was politically ambitious."

"That was a fairly recent phenomenon, though. Years ago, probably when I was in college, I remember him telling me that the last thing he wanted to do was hold any kind of governmental office."

"What changed his mind?"

"I'm not sure. Maybe he had gotten frustrated with what he saw as a lack of success that Three-G had against the mob. At least that's my impression."

"Did your mother encourage his interest in being governor?"

"I'm not sure that she cared one way or the other, although if he had become governor, I know she would have moved with him to that mansion up in Albany. After all, being first lady of New York State would have given her a much bigger platform from which to push her charities.

"And before you ask whether she knew about my father's amorous activities, the answer is . . . I don't know. I've assumed she did, but she has always been extremely self-contained, rarely showing much emotion, even to her children. I have heard her described as icy, although I don't happen to agree with that assessment. I prefer to say she is extremely reserved. She and I have always had a good relationship, although not an overly affectionate one."

"What is your impression of Weldon Dunagan?" I asked.

"For starters, he puts his money where his mouth is. He hates the crime syndicate as much as my father did, and he insisted on bankrolling the Good Government Group even though I think Daddy might have had more than enough money to finance it himself. As to Dunagan, I personally never have liked the man. I find him to be cold, unfeeling."

"But he and your father got along well?"

"As far as I could tell. One area where they seemed to differ was that Dunagan was somewhat more critical of the New York Police Department than Daddy."

"It seems he is out to get Inspector Cramer of Homicide in particular."

"Yes, I heard or read that, although I'm not sure where. Daddy always had fairly good relations with the police, but then, he also had a much more winning personality than Weldon Dunagan. He wasn't out to pick fights, although he was critical of the cops sometimes, too."

"Would you say Dunagan is out to pick fights?"

"That's how it seems to me, but you have to bear in mind that I am just an observer. I'm not privy to high-level conversations and machinations, nor do I want to be. There, how do you like that word, machinations?"

"I am impressed."

"As you should be. Well, Archie, I am afraid I do not have any more to tell you, unless you think I've left something out or am trying to hide a key piece of information from you."

"I don't think anything of the sort," I said with what Lily Rowan refers to as my winning grin.

"I am happy to hear that," Marianne said as she slid out of the booth, leaving a half-empty glass. "And thank you so much for the drinks. Unfortunately, I have to go back to work now. We're closing an edition of the magazine, and it's going to be a zoo across the street in our offices."

"Shouldn't you have something to eat?"

"You are very kind to ask, but one of the few really good things our company does is to bring in some decent foods on the nights we're putting the book to bed. And don't worry about my having had two drinks, well, almost two drinks. I hold my liquor extremely well." With that, she glided smoothly out of the bar and went through the revolving door into the Midtown night.

CHAPTER 17

By the time I got back to the brownstone, Wolfe had long since finished dining and was at his desk reading with beer as his companion. I started to report, but he insisted that first I go to the kitchen, where Fritz was keeping a plate of tonight's dinner warm for me, veal birds in casserole. If Wolfe were to have a motto to live by, it would be "Food first, work later."

Pleasantly full, I returned to the office and began to give Wolfe a verbatim report on my meeting with Marianne Pierce when the phone rang. It was Lon Cohen of the *Gazette*.

"If you and your boss have a few free minutes right now, I would like to read to you the lead item in Chad Preston's East Side, West Side, All Around the Town column that will run in tomorrow's edition." (A note here: The daily Preston column, probably the best-read feature in the *Gazette*, is a mixture of gossip, anonymous tips, and cheeky observations about life in

New York.) I nodded to Wolfe to pick up his telephone. "We are both on the line," I told Lon.

"Okay, here it is," he said:

> *Word around Gotham is that the rank and file in the police department is clamoring for the return of Inspector Lionel T. Cramer, who has for reasons unknown been put on the shelf by Commissioner O'Hara pending a decision on his future. Cramer's acting replacement in the Homicide Bureau, Captain George Rowcliff, has proven ineffective and has alienated staff members at all levels throughout One Police Plaza with his arrogance and dictatorial attitudes. The widely respected Cramer, probably the best department head in the recent history of the department, was not available for comment, nor was Commissioner O'Hara, who, according to an aide, is vacationing on a Caribbean island. When your scribe asked this aide if any progress is being made in the hunt for the killer of civic leader Lester Pierce, I received a terse "no comment" as well as a hang-up. Perhaps Mr. O'Hara should return from luxuriating in his island paradise and teach manners to both his aide and to Captain Rowcliff.*

"That's it," Lon said. "What do you think?"

"I am curious as to the source of Mr. Preston's item," Wolfe said.

"I'm afraid I can't help you there," Lon replied. "Chad protects his sources every bit as closely as Fort Knox guards its stash of gold. If I were to ask him where he got the item, he would tell me to—never mind what he would tell me. It would not be fit to print or to even repeat over the telephone."

"Just so," Wolfe said, hanging up his instrument.

"I appreciate your giving us the item," I told Lon.

"Have you got anything to give me in return, Archie?"

"Not at the moment. But we will be in touch."

"So you say. Just remember who your friends are."

"How can I forget? You won't let me," I said as we signed off.

Turning to Wolfe, I said, "I have an idea about who placed that item in Preston's column."

"You have no idea whatever!" Wolfe snapped, a beat too quickly.

"Okay, so I have no idea. Pardon me for thinking out loud in your presence. Go back to your book," I told him. "It's a nice evening for November. I'm headed out for a stroll to clear my mind."

Wolfe did not respond, and when I returned home from my walk over to the Hudson and back, he had gone to bed.

I spent much of the next morning after breakfast catching up on office work: typing up correspondence, updating the orchid germination records, and paying the grocery, heating, telephone, electric, and beer bills. When Wolfe came down from the plant rooms at eleven, he asked as usual if I had slept well, and I replied in the affirmative. Just as he got settled and buzzed for beer, the telephone rang, and I answered it with my usual spiel.

"Is Mr. Wolfe there?" It was a cultured female voice.

When I asked who was calling, she replied, "Audra Kingston Pierce," spacing the words and giving them equal stress.

"Just a moment, I will see if he is available," I said, scribbling her name on a sheet and handing it to Wolfe, who picked up his phone while I stayed on the line.

"This is Nero Wolfe."

"Mr. Wolfe, I am Audra Kingston Pierce." Again the words were carefully spaced. "May I assume you recognize my name?"

"You may."

"I should like to come and see you, at your convenience, of course."

"For what purpose, madam?" Wolfe asked.

"I would like to discuss my husband's death, and I know that you have an interest in that sad event. I spoke to my daughter by telephone on another matter this morning, and she told me that she and her brothers all have been interviewed by your Mr. Goodwin about the murder."

"That is correct."

"May I inquire as to whether you are working on behalf of someone?"

"I happen to have an interest in the case," he said, adding nothing more.

"As you would expect, so do I, and I would very much like to see you."

Wolfe's mug bore a slightly strained expression. He looked at me, and I nodded vigorously. "Very well," he said, "can you be at my home tonight at nine?"

"I can," the lady replied. "I believe I have your address." She read it off, and Wolfe told her she had it right.

"Things are about to get interesting," I said to Wolfe after we had hung up. He did not react, probably because he was seething about his upcoming conversation with Mrs. Pierce. He is not enthusiastic about having women in the brownstone, although he makes an exception for Lily Rowan, maybe because the first time I brought her to meet him, her opening request was to see his orchids. And on many successive visits, he has welcomed her with what for him passes as enthusiasm.

I have been known to needle Wolfe about his general aversion to women, and on one occasion, his reaction was, "Not like women? They are astonishing and successful animals." Another time, he said, "Not that I disapprove of women, except when they attempt to function as domestic animals. When they stick to the vocations for which they are best adapted, such as chicanery, sophistry, self-advertisement, cajolery, mystification, and incubation, they are sometimes superb creatures." So it was that I perversely looked forward to the evening's visit from Audra Kingston Pierce, and I was not to be disappointed.

At five minutes before nine, our bell rang, and I went to the front door to admit Mrs. Pierce. Behind her in the darkness, a Lincoln limousine idled at the curb, but I paid it scant interest. It was the lady who commanded my attention.

She was fifty-five. I knew that because of the information I had received about her. But I had a hard time believing that number. From her face, it was obvious she and Marianne were related, but if you were to see them side by side, you would swear they were sisters. And if she'd had some facial work done, it was skillful. Under an open mink stole, Audra was clad in a maroon blouse-and-skirt combination with matching purse and pumps. She had the figure of a coed, or at least of many of the college-age girls I had known in my checkered past.

"May I assume you to be Mr. Goodwin?" she asked, giving me the hint of a smile.

"You may, Mrs. Pierce. Please come in."

I held the door as she walked smoothly in and handed me her mink before I could help her off with it. After hanging the fur on the coatrack, I led her down the hall to the office, where she headed directly for the red leather chair as if sensing it was meant for her. She nodded and said to her host, "Mr. Wolfe." If she was surprised at his dimensions, she did not show it.

"Mrs. Pierce," he said with the slightest nod. "Can we get you something to drink? As you see, I am having beer."

"I would like a scotch on the rocks, single malt if you have it," she said, crossing one leg over the other. That move was not lost on Wolfe who, however much he may profess to be leery of women, invariably appreciates good legs—and Audra Kingston Pierce's legs were very shapely indeed.

I delivered her drink, a single malt scotch that Saul Panzer had once pronounced the best that had ever tickled his taste buds. And Saul knows his libations.

"I appreciate your agreeing to see me, particularly on such short notice," our guest said, brushing a nonexistent strand of blondish hair from her forehead.

"You have the floor, as well as my full attention and Mr. Goodwin's."

"Thank you. First of all, I must be totally candid with you, as I am not one to beat around the bush. I'm extremely curious as to why you have been investigating my husband's death. I am not aware that you knew him."

"I did not," Wolfe said. "My reasons for an interest in his murder are complex, and I choose not to elaborate on them at present."

"I see. May I assume you feel that Lester's death did not come at the hands of the crime syndicate?"

"I would not make that assumption, madam."

"You hold your cards very close, don't you?" she said before sampling the scotch and nodding. "All right, I will rephrase a question I asked you on the telephone: Do you have a client?"

"I do not, although Mr. Goodwin has been informing people, including your offspring, that we have a client who chooses to remain anonymous."

"Would you like to have a client?"

"That depends on a number of circumstances. Are you offering to engage me?"

"I am."

"Before we go any further, I would like to know your attitude about the police investigation."

"It has been absolutely pathetic," she said, waving the subject aside with a manicured hand. "That man—what's his name . . . Rowcliff—is a jackass, plain and simple. He doesn't seem to have the foggiest idea what he's doing, at least based on the conversations I have had with him. As far as I can tell, and read in the papers, the police have made no progress whatever."

Wolfe took a deep breath. "I will ask you the question you posed to me: Do you think organized crime was behind the death of your husband?"

"I . . . just don't know," Audra said. "I suppose it's understandable to conceive of them wanting him out of the way."

"You seem unsure about the syndicate involvement in the murder. Do you have any other candidates?"

Now it was her turn to breathe deeply. "No, I really do not. But I guess the reason I am, as you say, *unsure*, is that for all of the Good Government Group's railing against the evils of the mob, the group never seemed to me to pose a real threat to organized crime. I know that Lester was frustrated by Three-G's lack of success against them."

"Are you aware of any other enemies your husband had?"

She shook her head. "No, I am not. But, Mr. Wolfe, you should know that my husband and I did not have what you would call an overly intimate marriage, particularly in the last few years. We had grown apart, both of us being so deeply involved in our own projects. So I really can't say who might recently have come to dislike Lester enough to have him killed."

"Yet you care enough to consider hiring me to investigate his murder?"

"Yes, although it would be stretching the truth to say I still loved Lester, I want to see justice done, to use a trite phrase. After all, he was my husband right up to the end of his life. And money is no object," she said, pulling out a checkbook. "You may name a figure."

"We are getting ahead of ourselves," Wolfe cautioned. "If I am to take your case, you must understand my conditions. My findings might not satisfy you, for a variety of reasons. Perhaps I will conclude that the crime syndicate was indeed behind the murder. Or perhaps my findings will prove to be of great embarrassment to your husband, and by extension, to you. Also, I expect total candor. You may find some of my questions to be offensive, intrusive, or even downright rude. Diplomacy has never been my strong suit. However, I cannot be constrained in any way."

"I shall take my chances," Audra said firmly. "You will not find me difficult to deal with; I am prepared to pay whatever you ask, whether it be all up front or in the form of an initial retainer. I am not familiar with the financial intricacies of dealing with a private investigator."

"Let us start with a check for twenty-five thousand dollars," Wolfe said, "as, to use your term, an initial retainer. I will expect another payment of the same amount upon completion of my work."

"Those terms are quite agreeable to me," our new client said as she pulled an elegant fountain pen from her purse and wrote out a check, laying it carefully on the corner of Wolfe's desk as if it were a sacred gift from the Magi. "Now, where do we begin?"

"First, if I am asked whether I have a client, I assume you prefer that your name not be revealed."

"You are correct. I am not seeking personal publicity, rather the contrary."

"Agreed. Did your husband work well with other employees at the Good Government Group?" Wolfe asked.

"He seemed to, as far as I could tell. He did not talk to me much at all about his work. As I told you earlier, we were living increasingly separate lives."

"Who will take over his leadership at the organization?"

"I suppose it will be Roland Marchbank, although I have not heard anything about that. As you probably know, he has been Lester's second in command for several years."

"What is your opinion of Mr. Marchbank?"

"Where to start? Roland is . . . well, hardly what you would term 'Mr. Sunshine.' He is dour by nature, I suppose. He always seemed to me to be a strange choice to be the number two person at Three-G, but Lester apparently was comfortable having him there."

"Would you term Mr. Marchbank ambitious?" Wolfe asked.

Audra gave him a thin, mirthless smile. "Ambitious? Yes, I would say so, definitely. In my mind, there was no question that he coveted my husband's job. I also happen to know from acquaintances that on occasion he bad-mouthed Lester to other people."

"In what way?"

"He was heard to say things like 'Oh, Lester is a fine guy all right, but his mind isn't really on Three-G these days. He wants to be governor so badly he can already picture himself in that Albany mansion.'"

"Do you concur with that assessment?"

"I concur with half of Roland's comment, that Lester really did want to be governor, and very badly, although he did not broadcast the fact to many people. More than once, though, he said to me things like 'I really believe I can solve many of the state's problems.'

"As to whether he had lost interest in Three-G, I never got that impression at all. I think Roland hoped his comments would somehow get back to Weldon Dunagan, who might then question Lester's commitment."

"Did your husband enjoy amicable relations with Mr. Dunagan?"

"Yes, from everything I was able to see. As I'm sure you are aware, Weldon financed the Good Government Group's operations. He detests the crime syndicate, and Lester shared his passion. Weldon was the first person to visit me after the shooting—even before my children stopped by. He seemed terribly torn up about what happened, and he is not by nature an emotional individual."

"Did Mr. Dunagan voice any thoughts as to who was behind the killing?" Wolfe asked.

"From the way he talked—and he was very angry—there was no doubt that he was puzzled as to who did the shooting. He did not seem to think it was the mob. 'Somehow we will get them, whoever they are, Audra, I promise you that,' he said to me."

Wolfe drank the last of his beer and dabbed his lips with a handkerchief. "Other than Mr. Marchbank, are you aware of any other candidates who might replace your husband at the Good Government Group?"

Audra looked at me and nodded toward her empty glass. I took it and went for a refill as she turned back to Wolfe. "I was wondering how long before you asked that question," she told him in a voice that was neither friendly nor hostile. "I am sure the name Laura Cordwell is familiar to you."

"I have heard it but have yet to meet the woman."

"Very diplomatic. I could continue asking what you know about her, but I have the distinct feeling that would be a waste of time, and I have not come here to waste either your time or mine. Laura's official title at Three-G has been assistant to the executive director, but she has been much more than that, as many people are aware, you among them, I suspect."

She did not wait for a response from Wolfe but moved ahead. "Laura came to Three-G three years ago after getting a graduate business degree from Columbia, and she wasted no time ingratiating herself with Lester. Of course, it did not hurt her cause that she had been in the Miss America competition a few years earlier. Oh, dear, I suppose that now I sound like a jealous wife, don't I?" she said, putting her hand to her lips in a stagey gesture.

When Wolfe chose to make no reply, Audra continued after a pause.

"It was not long before Laura had made herself all but indispensable in the Three-G structure. Her relationship with Lester became the subject of much speculation, as I was to learn from 'friends.' I find it amazing how eager some people are to deliver news that might be found disturbing to the recipient. Sadistic comes to mind. Anyway, I pretended to ignore the situation, but Laura's closeness to Lester—surely in more ways than one—got under Roland Marchbank's skin, or so I was told by one of those so-called friends I referred to earlier. Roland felt, correctly, that the former beauty queen was supplanting him as Lester's trusted right-hand . . . person."

"Such a situation might well exacerbate any tensions in the organization's office," Wolfe observed.

"That is putting it mildly," Audra said.

"Has Mr. Dunagan spoken to you since he visited to offer his condolences?"

"No, although he hasn't had any reason to. Lester's memorial service will not be held for several weeks. I am sure I will see him there."

"I recall in a news article on your husband's death, Mr. Dunagan had been quoted as calling for the removal of Inspector

Cramer from the Homicide Squad. Are you aware of any rancor between them?"

"No, I am not. I do know that Dunagan has it in for Cramer, and I am not sure why. And he had encouraged Lester to attack the inspector at every opportunity. And Lester did, being a good soldier."

"Do you have any other information you feel might be helpful?"

Audra looked at the ceiling as if considering the question. "No . . . I do not believe so. How do you plan to proceed?"

"With diligence, perseverance, and inspiration," Wolfe said.

"You do not lack for self-confidence, do you?"

"Madam, I know what I am capable of, and I do not embrace the indulgence of false modesty. Now if you will excuse me," he said, rising, "I have other business that needs attention." He walked out and down the hall.

Audra turned to me. "That was a somewhat abrupt departure," she remarked with a crooked smile.

"It was nothing you said," I told her. "Mr. Wolfe is not one for small talk."

"I can appreciate that. Neither am I. May I trust that you will keep me apprised of developments?"

"You may. In fact, you probably will hear from me more often than from Mr. Wolfe," I said as I walked her to the front hall, where I helped her on with her mink. The limousine that had brought our guest to the brownstone awaited her at the curb. I assumed it had been there throughout her visit.

After watching the big car pull smoothly away, I relocked the front door and walked down the hall to the kitchen, where I knew I would find Wolfe. The "other business" he referred to as he left the office was the usual planning session with Fritz over the luncheon and dinner menus for the week ahead.

CHAPTER 18

I walked into the kitchen to find Wolfe and Fritz standing and glaring at each other on either side of the big cutting board. Clearly an argument of some kind was under way. It might have been over chives or leeks or basil or oregano or onions or any number of other ingredients, but I did not wait to find out. No good could come from my trying to serve as a referee, so I went up to bed.

The next morning after breakfast, I ambled into the office with coffee and found a handwritten note on my desk:

> A.G.
> Please arrange to have Roland Marchbank here
> as soon as possible, preferably tonight.
> N.W.

That brief bit of correspondence nicely summarizes my relationship with Nero Wolfe: He gives orders, I deliver. That is how it has been for years, and it is unlikely to ever change. My boss rarely makes suggestions as to how I am to make something happen; he simply issues a directive.

I called the Good Government Group's office and got the same young man who had answered when I telephoned asking for Laura Cordwell. I gave my name and told him whom I wanted to speak to—and why.

"Yes, I recognize your voice. I will transfer you."

"Yes, what is it?" Marchbank barked. The man must have learned his telephone etiquette from my boss.

I gave my name, reminding him that Nero Wolfe was looking into Pierce's murder. "Mr. Wolfe would like to talk to you at his office," I added.

"Look, your man Panzer has already talked to me. What more would be accomplished by my seeing Wolfe?" he snarled.

"Are you happy with how the police have been progressing on Mr. Pierce's killing?"

"Of course not."

"Then what have you got to lose by seeing Nero Wolfe?"

"I am absolutely swamped here without Lester." His voice had now taken on a whine.

"Let me read your quote that ran in the *New York Times* the day after Lester Pierce's murder: 'We at the Good Government Group will not rest until the perpetrator of this brazen crime is brought to justice.' Do you still feel that way?"

The response was silence for at least thirty seconds, followed by an extended sigh. "All right," Marchbank said grudgingly. "Just when does this man Wolfe want to see me?"

"Tonight, preferably at nine o'clock."

"What! That is damned short notice."

"I am sure you are as anxious as we are to find Mr. Pierce's killer."

"All right, all right, you have made your point. Give me the address." I did and told him we would expect him at nine. His response was to hang up without comment.

After Wolfe came down from the plant rooms, settled in, and rang for beer, I reported on my conversation with Marchbank. "He says he will be here tonight, but he's not in the least happy about it."

"We are not seeking to make him happy, Archie. Can you reach Mr. Cohen on the telephone?"

"I'm sure I can at this hour, why?"

"Just call him."

I dialed one of the many numbers I knew by heart, and Lon answered on the second ring. "Mr. Wolfe would like to talk to you," I said, staying on the line.

"Hello, Mr. Cohen," Wolfe said. "Would the *Gazette* be interested in an article about my looking into the death of Lester Pierce?"

"Of course we would."

"Will you have a reporter interview me?"

"Reporter, hell, I'll do it myself. I haven't forgotten how to write a news story, and this definitely is news, although I am not surprised that you've decided to make your involvement official. Tell me what you want to say."

"Very well. After thoughtful consideration, I have decided to undertake an investigation into the shooting death of Lester Pierce, one of New York's most highly respected civic leaders. I have no suspects at present, and my investigation is to be financed by an anonymous client. Do you have enough to construct an article?"

"I can flesh it out a bit, although I do have a question," Lon said. "What made you decide to accept this commission?"

"I feel there has been a marked lack of progress in the official investigation."

"Would you like to include a quote that is critical of the police?"

"No, I would not. I believe my 'marked lack of progress' comment speaks for itself."

"All right. Anything else you wish to add?"

"No. I would like the finished version read back to me."

"That will be done. I should have something within the hour."

"I await your call," Wolfe said, hanging up.

"Well, I will be damned," I said. "I did not see that coming. You threw me a curveball."

"I recall you told me once that as a youth playing baseball, you were adept at hitting curveballs," Wolfe replied, a corner of his mouth twitching. This is one of his versions of a smile.

"That was years ago, when I was young and possessed great reflexes. Things have a way of sneaking up on me now. What do you hope to accomplish with this *Gazette* article?"

"We will see. And if I know Mr. Cohen, he will have written something within the hour."

Within the half hour was more like it. When the phone rang, I figured it was Lon and I figured right. I nodded to Wolfe, who picked up his phone and motioned me to stay on the line.

"All right, Mr. Wolfe, here it is. Tell me what you think."

Nero Wolfe, the well-known New York private detective, today announced that he has begun an investigation into the death of Lester Pierce, the head of the watchdog Good Government Group. Mr. Pierce was gunned down in front of his Park Avenue co-op more than two weeks ago. Paragraph. Mr. Wolfe, who declined to name his client, told the Gazette *he was stimulated to take action in the case because of what he called, quote, a marked lack of progress in the official investigation into the death of Mr. Pierce end quote. The well-known civic leader, 56, had headed the group popularly known as Three-G for six years. When asked by the* Gazette *for his reaction to Mr. Wolfe's entry into the investigation, New York Police Commissioner Daniel J. O'Hara declined to comment.*

"That's it," Lon said.

"Will the headline contain my name?" Wolfe asked.

"Yes, and your picture as well. The headline reads 'Noted Detective Nero Wolfe Jumps into Pierce Case.' The piece will run on page three and the presses are about to start rolling with your okay. The first copies should be on the street in half an hour," Lon said.

"Satisfactory," Wolfe said, hanging up as I stayed on the line. "All right, don't say we never do anything for you," I told Lon.

"Heaven forbid. I have no doubt that your boss will crack this Pierce business wide open, and I am sure that when that happens, the *Gazette* will be the first to know, right?"

"Smell a scoop, do you, typewriter cowpoke? Well, just hold your horses, because this could be a long haul. And I have a feeling things are going to get wild around the brownstone once your piece about Wolfe hits the streets."

"You are about to see the power of the press at work," Lon said. "It cannot be overestimated. Prepare yourself."

Lon Cohen was correct, and not for the first time. Just after we finished lunch and had gotten settled at our desks in the office with coffee, the bell rang, again and again. Someone was insistent. I walked down the hall and through the one-way glass in the door saw an individual I had hoped never to lay eyes on again. I retraced my steps and returned to the office, standing in the doorway.

"We have an unexpected visitor," I told Wolfe, "none other than your old friend, Captain George Rowcliff. Should I let him stand there until his finger gets tired or open the door and tell him to buy a one-way ticket to Saskatoon?"

"Neither, Archie," he said offhandedly. "Invite the gentleman in." As much as it pained me, I followed orders and swung the door open for our angry visitor. "Whatever you're selling, we don't need any," I told Rowcliff.

"I want to see Wolfe, and I want to see him now!" he rasped, his eyes bulging as they often do when he is angry.

"All right, all right, don't get snippy about it," I said, holding open the door. He barged past me much as Cramer has done so many times, striding down the hall with me trailing in his wake.

"So, you are meddling in police business once again!" Rowcliff growled as he parked in the red leather chair without an invitation to sit. "Maybe you could get away with your high-handed tactics before, but not now that I am in charge."

"Mr. Rowcliff, I did not realize you had been anointed as the permanent head of the Homicide Squad," Wolfe said, eyebrows raised.

Rowcliff's ears turned red and his eyes began to bulge again. "I know you're out to get me—both of you," he yelped, turning in my direction and then glaring back at Wolfe. "I also know that you're the ones w-who planted that da-damned item in Chad Preston's sleazy *Gazette* column." He had begun to stutter, as he does when he gets flustered.

"Whether you choose to believe it or not, sir, neither Mr. Goodwin nor I had anything to do with that mention in the *Gazette.*"

"Huh! So you claim," Rowcliff retorted. "Well, the main reason I came here is to tell you to st-stay out of my way, or by heaven, I will see that your licenses get pulled. You have gotten away with high-handed tactics in the past, but those days are over now, and the sooner you realize that, the bet-bet-better."

"Are you finished?" Wolfe asked as Rowcliff got to his feet abruptly and turned toward the door.

"Quite finished," the cop said over his shoulder. "I hope that I have seen the last of you two."

I started to reply in kind, but as he so often does, Wolfe read my mind and held up a hand to stifle me. So, biting my tongue, I followed Rowcliff down the hall and closed and locked the front door behind him as he went down the steps to an unmarked car that sat at the curb.

"I knew precisely what you were going to say to the departing officer, and I can hardly blame you," Wolfe said. "However, we will surely have an opportunity in the near future to take our angry visitor down a peg."

"I live for that moment. By the way, I know I did not talk to that *Gazette* columnist Preston, and you said you didn't, so . . ."

Wolfe closed his eyes and murmured, "I understand Saul to be on friendly terms with Mr. Preston."

CHAPTER 19

I had plenty to tell Wolfe that evening when he descended from the plant rooms at six, as a lot had happened during his two-hour playtime with those three climate-controlled rooms full of orchids. I waited until after he had gotten settled at his desk with beer before bombarding him.

"That piece about you in the *Gazette* got a lot of attention," I told him. "While you were having fun up on the roof, I was busy answering the telephone. News hawks from the *Times*, *Daily News*, *Post*, *Herald Tribune*, and *Journal-American* all wanted to talk to you, and some of them, including the guy from the *Times* who had spoken to you earlier, were damned persistent. But I told them all the same thing: 'Mr. Wolfe is not available, and I don't know when he will be.' In a couple of cases, I simply had to hang up."

Wolfe's response was to open his current book and begin reading.

"No comment on any of that, eh? All right, try this one on for size: Police Commissioner O'Hara also called, and to say he was furious would be an understatement. He demanded that you come to his office and explain what you're up to. I gave him the company line: 'Mr. Wolfe has a hard-and-fast policy never to leave home on business.' Of course that did not satisfy him, and he said he would call again. Somehow, he knows enough about you to realize that every day from nine to eleven in the morning and four to six in the afternoon you are sequestered with the orchids.

"That's the price of fame, I suppose. Anyway, the chances are Mr. O'Hara will be calling again, probably very soon." I had barely gotten those words out when the telephone rang.

"All right, Goodwin," the commissioner harrumphed after I had answered in the usual way. "I know that your boss is in. He's always in or else playing with those damned flowers of his. Put him on!"

"Just a moment, sir, I will see if he is available," I replied, cupping the phone and mouthing *O'Hara* to Wolfe, who scowled and picked up his receiver while I stayed on the line.

"This is Nero Wolfe."

"And as I'm sure your assistant has told you, this is Police Commissioner Daniel J. O'Hara, and I want to see you."

"For what purpose, sir?"

"Don't try to get cute with me, Wolfe; it won't wash. Just remember this and remember it well: I can get your license lifted with one phone call, as well as that of your flunky Goodwin."

"And for what reason?"

"Getting in the way of a police investigation, something I should be used to from you by now."

"I fail to see how I have in any way impeded the work of your department," Wolfe said evenly.

O'Hara snorted. "You know damned well what I'm talking about."

"I am afraid I do not, sir."

"As I said before, I want to see you. Your man tells me you never leave home on business, and as I just said, by now I should be used to your eccentric behavior. But bear in mind that this is not the era of Skinner and Cramer any longer."

"So I have been led to understand. Whatever the era, however, I see no reason to leave my home to indulge you. If you remain insistent upon a face-to-face meeting, I will be available here tomorrow at nine in the evening. I am sure you have the address."

"Pretty high-handed, aren't you?"

"I tend to respond in kind. Shall I expect you at nine?"

The commissioner uttered a phrase not worth repeating, but followed that by grumbling, "I will be there" and hung up.

"So now I'm a flunky? Is that better or worse than a lackey, as I also have been called by one or more members of the police over the years?"

Wolfe ignored my questions, which is hardly unusual. "So, do I have any instructions?" I asked.

"Not at the moment, other than to continue keeping those newspaper reporters at bay. Tell them I am not available, nor will I be until further notice."

"Well, my goodness, those words will surely keep them happy." Once again I got ignored, but I pushed on. "Care to tell me what the strategy is with Marchbank tonight?"

"We shall take the measure of the man and see of what stuff he is made," Wolfe said, returning to his book.

That shut me up, so I went to the kitchen to see how Fritz was progressing with the dinner preparations.

■ ■ ■

At two minutes to nine that night, the doorbell rang. March-bank was prompt, which was a point in his favor. As I let him in, his face was fixed in a frown—a point against. I hung up his coat and gave him the once-over. Both Lily's and Saul's descriptions of the man came back to me: short, dark-haired, and wearing what seems to be a permanent scowl.

They had failed to mention his most prominent feature, however: bushy black eyebrows in need of a trimming that gave him a fierce look. I was impressed by his charcoal three-piece suit, though. *At least he has some taste*, I thought as I led him down the hall to the office.

He parked himself in the red leather chair and glared at Wolfe, who ignored the facial expression. "Good evening, sir, will you have something to drink? As you see, my choice is beer."

"I didn't realize this was a social call, but—oh, why not. Have you got rye?"

"We do," I said. "With water or a mix or on the rocks?"

"Rocks." I went to the serving cart as Marchbank spoke to Wolfe. "All right, you've got me here now. I answered all of your man Panzer's questions, and I don't know what more I can tell you. What's the play here?"

"The play, sir, is that I am engaged in finding the killer of Lester Pierce, as you may already know from Mr. Panzer."

"Yes, and he couldn't—or didn't—tell me who engaged you, and I would like to know the identity of that individual," he demanded.

"That detail is not a part of this discussion."

"Is that so? Just why all the secrecy?"

"Does not knowing my client's identity concern you?"

"I guess it shouldn't," Marchbank said, shrugging. "My main interest is to see Lester's murderer caught."

"Do you have any thoughts as to who that might be?"

Marchbank ran a hand through his thick mop of hair. "On the surface, the crime syndicate would seem to be the obvious answer," he said, although he did not sound convinced.

"Can you with certainty state that either Mr. Pierce or the Good Government Group has posed a serious threat to organized crime in this city?" Wolfe asked.

"I like to think we have frustrated their operations," our guest replied stiffly.

"Can you cite specific accomplishments?"

Marchbank shifted in his chair. "Several of the newspapers have praised our efforts."

"But have mob activities been substantially curtailed or hampered?"

"I would have to say no."

"That also has been my impression," Wolfe said, "which makes me wonder what the crime syndicate would have to gain by killing Mr. Pierce."

"That thought had also occurred to me," Marchbank said, "although the shooting sure as hell had all the earmarks of a mob hit."

"You were Mr. Pierce's right-hand man. Have you been anointed his successor?"

"No, that will be up to Weldon Dunagan, and he is probably waiting to make an announcement until after Lester's memorial service."

"Do you have any doubt that you will be the individual selected to run the organization?"

"How much do you know about the inner workings of Three-G?"

"Very little," Wolfe said. "Please enlighten me."

Marchbank leaned back in the chair and stretched his arms over his head. The drink had begun to mellow the man. "Well, for starters, Dunagan really underwrites the whole operation, as you probably are aware." Wolfe dipped his chin, which Marchbank took as a signal to continue.

"Anyway, Dunagan pretty much gave Lester carte blanche in the running of Three-G. And it is important to remember that we don't just go after organized crime, we also investigate corrupt behavior in local governmental agencies, and in at least two instances, we have been instrumental in getting city department heads removed from their jobs. Also, in one case a crooked building inspector was sent to jail because of our diligence."

"Does the Good Government Group have a staff of investigators?" Wolfe asked.

"If three people constitute a staff, we do," Marchbank said, allowing himself the hint of a smile. "But then I shouldn't demean them; they're damned hardworking. And we do have a team of highly motivated and idealistic recent college graduates who also help in the investigations as interns."

"Other than you, are there others at the management level of the organization?"

"Of course there's Laura Cordwell, whose title was assistant to Lester. Have you talked to her?"

"I have not met the lady," Wolfe said, neglecting to mention my session with her.

"She is quite ambitious, to say the least."

"Would she be a candidate to succeed Mr. Pierce?"

Marchbank made a derisive sound. "I am sure she feels that she would be an ideal candidate. At the risk of sounding petty, I have found her to be more than a little duplicitous. She had seemed to take delight in trying to block my access to Lester."

"Was she successful?"

"Sometimes, not always. She enjoyed what you might call a 'special relationship' with him, if you get my drift."

"Was this relationship common knowledge?" Wolfe asked.

"It was hardly secret. I was very disappointed with Lester, but then, he had had other . . . liaisons in the past, or so I had been led to believe."

"Was Mr. Dunagan aware of the presumed amour between two of the staff?"

"I honestly don't know, but I doubt it. This much I can tell you: He would not have learned about it from me. I refuse to deal in office gossip," Marchbank said, his voice assuming a self-righteous tone. "My only concern has been the success of Three-G."

"If for some reason you are not selected as Mr. Pierce's successor, would you remain in the organization?"

"I would have to think about it," he said after taking a deep breath. "Although I don't see how that is pertinent in a discussion of Lester's murder."

"Perhaps it is not," Wolfe conceded, "although I pose the question to gauge your commitment to the Good Government Group."

"I could choose to be insulted by that, but I won't. Whether or not I stay with Three-G, I will always be supportive of their work."

"How would you describe your relationship with Mr. Dunagan?"

"We've always gotten along well, although he and I did not have a lot of direct contact with Lester in charge. I believe he feels that I am good at my job, though. I have gotten regular raises."

"Have the two of you had any conversations since Mr. Pierce's death?"

"We have not," Marchbank said. "Again, everything will be pretty much on hold until after the memorial service, including any investigations that we've been undertaking."

"Speaking of investigations, do you have an opinion as to how the police are handling theirs with regard to the Pierce murder?"

"Huh! They seem to be getting nowhere, which is why I agreed to see you. Twice, I've talked to this captain—what's his name . . . Rowcliff—and I have been underwhelmed, if that's even a word. I don't have any idea how he got put in charge of the investigation."

"He is the acting head of the Homicide Squad, replacing Inspector Cramer," Wolfe said.

"Cramer, yes, I've heard of him, of course, but I've never worked with him during my time at Three-G. I always got the impression that he was a good man."

"There are many who believe that to be so."

"Well, for what it's worth, I am planning to complain about Rowcliff to Commissioner O'Hara, whom I've come to know through our work with the police at Three-G," Marchbank said.

"It will be instructive to get the commissioner's reaction," Wolfe said. "My understanding is that others have been critical of Mr. Rowcliff as well."

"Is that so?"

"Yes, sir, and a column item ran in one of the daily newspapers recently suggesting that many within the police department also are unhappy with the man and would like to see Mr. Cramer reinstated."

"I must have missed that, although I don't usually read the columns, I find them a waste of time. I have never had any direct dealings with Cramer, but as I just said, what I've heard about him has been generally positive. For some reason, though, Dunagan doesn't seem to like him. And, yes, I am definitely going to speak to O'Hara about Rowcliff. Now, if you have no further need of me, I must be going."

"Good evening, sir," Wolfe said. "Mr. Goodwin will show you out."

When I returned to the office after watching Marchbank descend the front steps and climb into his sedan at the curb, Wolfe's nose was buried in his book once again. I liked what he was doing, but I couldn't resist tweaking him nonetheless. "If I didn't know better, I might think you've been trying to foment trouble for Captain George Rowcliff. After all, Saul already had interviewed Marchbank, and it seemed that your main thrust tonight was to turn him against Rowcliff."

He looked up, his face expressionless, then returned to the book as if I had not spoken. I grinned, went to the kitchen for a glass of milk, and climbed the stairs to my room.

CHAPTER 20

I spent much of the next morning catching up on Wolfe's correspondence and the orchid germination records. At a quarter to eleven, I went out to the front stoop and picked up the *Gazette*. It's an afternoon paper, but they put out an early edition that gets delivered to the brownstone late each weekday morning. As had been my habit the last few days, I turned first to Chad Preston's chatty and acerbic East Side, West Side, All Around the Town column.

Saul, likely urged on by Wolfe, apparently had fed Preston another item:

Police Headquarters on Centre Street must have been rocking yesterday with the ranting of Captain George Rowcliff, who, according to sources on the force, is far out of his depth as interim head of the Homicide Squad. The cause of Rowcliff's tantrum, we are told, was the failure of an underling to show him the proper respect. This was just the latest in a series of outbursts by the captain. One member of the force tells us that "Mr. Rowcliff is in desperate need of psychiatric help." Word is that a group of senior officers plans to approach Commissioner O'Hara, urging him to reinstate the highly respected Inspector Lionel T. Cramer as head of Homicide. Cramer has been placed on administrative leave for unspecified reasons.

I folded the *Gazette* with Preston's column face-up and placed it on Wolfe's desk blotter. The only newspaper that he sees before coming down from the plant rooms in the morning is the *Times*, a copy of which Fritz takes up with his breakfast tray.

I was back at my desk working when Wolfe strode into the office and settled in at his desk. I watched over my shoulder as he picked up the *Gazette* and began reading. He did not smile, but he didn't frown either.

"Intriguing item," I said as he put the paper down and rang for beer.

"Yes, but I doubt very much that Mr. Rowcliff is intrigued by it."

"It will be particularly interesting to see how our evening visitor reacts to the Preston column."

"Mr. O'Hara will not be pleased, but that should not be of concern to us."

"You have never much liked O'Hara."

"I was not enthused about his predecessor either, Archie, but Mr. Skinner at least was possessed of a modicum of intelligence as commissioner, which is more than I can say for the man who has taken over."

"Is there a plan for this evening?"

Wolfe drank beer and set his glass down, licking his lips. "We will try our best to educate Mr. O'Hara regarding certain realities."

"Would one of these realities by chance concern Captain George Rowcliff?"

"It would," he replied, taking out his pen and signing the correspondence I had stacked on his desk. He had said all he was going to about tonight's visit from the police commissioner.

Like Marchbank had been the previous night, Daniel J. O'Hara was prompt, ringing our bell at three minutes to nine. I gave him a smile as I opened the front door and was rewarded with a frown. I took his homburg and overcoat and hung them on the rack, then directed him down the hall to the office.

"Mr. O'Hara," Wolfe said as our guest slid into the red leather chair and ran a hand over a full head of white hair that contrasted with the tan he had developed on his recent Caribbean trip.

"All right, Wolfe, I'm here, since you refuse to budge from this bunker of yours."

"Hardly a bunker, sir. Will you have something to drink?"

O'Hara screwed up his face and then relaxed it. "Oh, since I am indulging you by coming here, you can indulge me with a really good scotch, if you happen to have one."

Wolfe nodded at me and I went to the serving cart, coming back with three different bottles, which I showed to the commissioner.

"A poverty of riches," he said with the hint of a smile. "I'll take that one," he said, pointing at the most expensive label—"on the rocks."

Once O'Hara had sampled his drink, he turned to Wolfe with a frown. "Well?"

"Well what, sir?" Wolfe responded. "You requested this meeting."

"You're damned right I did. As I said on the telephone, you are getting in the way of a murder investigation."

"And as I responded during that call, neither I nor anyone in my employ has impeded the police investigation into the death of Lester Pierce."

"So you say. Captain Rowcliff has complained to me about you."

"Is that so?" Wolfe said. "What was the nature of the complaint?"

"He did not get specific, but he clearly was upset."

"Apparently, that is not an unusual state for Mr. Rowcliff."

"Look, the man is doing his best in a difficult situation," O'Hara said in a defensive tone.

"His best clearly does not appear to be sufficient. Have you considered that he is out of his depth in the position?"

"Don't tell me how to run my department!"

"I would not think of it," Wolfe said. "Are you satisfied with the progress being made in the Pierce investigation?"

"I am not here to discuss our progress. The subject is your meddling, which should not surprise anyone, given your track record in police work over the years."

"Again, sir, I ask you to point out examples of my meddling in police business."

"That article the other day in the *Gazette*, for example, where you said there had been, and I quote, 'a marked lack of progress in the official investigation into the death of Mr. Pierce.' That was a slap in the face to the police department."

"As I recall, the *Gazette* gave you the opportunity to respond to my comment, and you declined."

"I chose not to dignify your statement," O'Hara said stiffly.

"Or was it that you did not want to concede that little or no progress has been made in the investigation?"

"I find that to be offensive, Wolfe."

"I did not mean to give offense, only to pose an obvious question. Mr. O'Hara, both you and the department are in a bind, and—no, hear me out," Wolfe said as the commissioner started to interrupt.

"I have hardly been alone in criticizing the department in this instance. At least two newspapers have written editorials decrying your progress. I do not feel the blame, however, should be lain at your feet, at least not directly."

O'Hara gave a start, almost spilling some of the drink from the glass in his hand. "Then just where do you see the blame lain?"

"We are being candid with each other, sir. Anything less would be a waste of our time. It has become patently clear that Mr. Rowcliff is an inadequate leader of the Homicide Squad."

"You just don't like him; I am all too aware of that."

"It is not a case of like or dislike, but of leadership, and Mr. Rowcliff does not possess that quality."

"Are you saying this because of what that disreputable *Gazette* columnist Preston has been writing about him?"

"No, sir, I am not. I have had numerous occasions over the years to observe Mr. Rowcliff at work, and although I have never doubted his bravery, I have found him to be impulsive, erratic, temperamental, and quick to anger. Have you seen him inspire loyalty and respect among his troops?"

O'Hara was silent for several seconds before speaking. "I suppose you have a better idea?"

"Are you soliciting my opinion?" Wolfe asked.

More silence from the commissioner, then: "All right, yes, tell me what you think. You are going to anyway."

"I believe you, the department, and the city would be far better served if Inspector Cramer were reinstated."

"I can't do that!" O'Hara barked.

"Why not, sir?"

Our guest slumped in his chair and glanced at his empty glass, which I took from him and refilled. "This conversation must be off the record," he said in a voice just above a whisper, as if someone were eavesdropping.

"I am not known to be loose-tongued, nor is Mr. Goodwin," Wolfe replied.

"All right, I know Cramer has done a good job over the years—hell, a very good job on balance. I inherited him from Skinner, as you know, and although my original goal was to replace all the department heads, I hesitated getting rid of Cramer because of his reputation. But I was getting pressure . . ."

"From whom?"

O'Hara shifted and took a swallow of scotch, presumably to fortify himself. "Of course you know who Weldon Dunagan is," he said to Wolfe.

"I do, although I have yet to meet the man."

"You may not have met him, but you won't be surprised to learn that he wields a lot of power in town, and not just with that Good Government Group he underwrites. He just got a seat on the Police Review Board, and he does not like Cramer."

"Does he give a reason for his animus?"

"This is very hard to talk about," the commissioner said. "Some years ago, Dunagan's son got into trouble—I don't know all the details as I was just a lieutenant at the time—and Cramer had something to do with the boy's being found guilty of a felony in court and serving prison time."

"So Mr. Cramer has in effect become the victim of a vendetta undertaken by Weldon Dunagan," Wolfe stated.

"I would not put it that way."

"How would you put it?"

O'Hara was getting increasingly uncomfortable, and I felt some sympathy for him. Finally, he cleared his throat and spoke in a hoarse voice: "You can't possibly appreciate the pressure that I am under as commissioner."

"Perhaps that is so," Wolfe said, "but is it not a position that you actively aspired to?"

"That's true, and I am determined to do a good job of it, despite what you might think."

"Mr. O'Hara, I am not your enemy, nor do I intend to be. However, it stands to reason that the longer Mr. Rowcliff remains in his present position, the more difficult your own role will be. You may not like what has been written about the captain in that *Gazette* column, but I have yet to hear or read any denials coming from the department regarding the veracity of those reports."

"I can't just fire Rowcliff."

"Come, sir, you know very well that there are other ways of handling a personnel change, ways that can be face-saving for the individual being demoted. You certainly have had to make decisions like this in the past in your various management positions within the department."

"What if Cramer does not want to return? I am sure he's bitter over what has happened."

"There is but one way to find out," Wolfe told him. "You may well have to eat crow, but its taste will be short-lived, while the long-range benefits to you and to the department in general figure to be palatable."

O'Hara ran a hand over his forehead and stood. "All right, I cannot honestly say that this has been the most pleasant evening I have ever had, but at least the scotch was first-rate," he said, giving a grim nod in my direction. "Good night. I will see myself out."

When I returned to the office after watching the stony-faced O'Hara leave the brownstone and climb into a waiting car, I said to Wolfe: "That was an impressive performance. Within minutes of O'Hara's arrival, you had managed to smoothly switch the topic of conversation from your supposed meddling in police business to Rowcliff's ineptitude. Nice job."

"That remains to be seen," Wolfe said.

"Do you think O'Hara will reach out to Cramer?"

"Archie, you are the one who likes to give odds. You tell me."

"Okay, since you asked, I'm laying two to one that (a) O'Hara does make the call, and (b) Cramer agrees to go back to work."

CHAPTER 21

It did not take long the next morning for my odds-making skills to be put to the test. I was in the office after break-fast sipping coffee when I answered the telephone and was greeted by the voice of none other than the *Gazette*'s Lon Cohen.

"I know something that you don't know," he chortled.

"You mean you interrupted my morning reverie with that supposed nugget of information? Am I supposed to play a guessing game?"

"As much fun as that would be, I don't have the time."

"And you think I do?"

"Of course. Detectives don't have deadlines like us poor mortals. Anyway, I am going to read to you from a New York Police Department press release that came over the local wire just minutes ago. Under the headline 'Cramer Back Leading Homicide,' it reads:

Inspector Lionel T. Cramer has returned to his position as head of the Department's Homicide Squad, according to Police Commissioner Daniel J. O'Hara. "I am delighted to report that Inspector Cramer has returned to the helm of Homicide," Commissioner O'Hara said. "He has compiled a superb record over the years and is anxious to resume his duties. Captain George Rowcliff, who has done an admirable job of stepping in during Mr. Cramer's absence, will fill an important management role in the reorganized Traffic Division.

"How is that for news?" Lon said. "And the great thing is that it came out too late for any editions of the morning papers. We will play it on page one."

"This is good for Cramer, bad for Rowcliff. One question still needs to be answered, though," I said.

"Yeah, why did Cramer have dinner with Ralph Mars of crime syndicate fame? Maybe your boss can find that out."

"So he can feed it to you for a scoop?"

"I didn't say that, but . . ."

"So there you go, getting greedy again."

"It's an occupational hazard. Hell, a guy can try, can't he?"

"I would begin to worry about you if you didn't at least try," I said. "But I'd advise you not to hold your breath on this one. It's likely the truth may never come out about that dinner."

"I disagree. I think it will. And if that happens, I hope it doesn't damage the inspector too much. I know he's ornery and cantankerous, but we're all used to dealing with him."

"Ornery? Cantankerous? It sounds like you're describing my boss."

"Now just what would Nero Wolfe say if he heard you talking like that?"

"He's heard me call him those before—and a lot of other adjectives just as descriptive."

"Well, now that it's official you two are working on the Pierce murder—as reported in a *Gazette* exclusive—I know that you will keep me in mind whenever there are developments our readers would like to learn about."

"Back atcha. Conversely, Mr. Wolfe and I know that if you find anything of interest, you will pick up the telephone and call us."

"Conversely, huh? Being around Wolfe for so long has done wonders for your vocabulary."

"I'm a quick learner. Talk to you later."

When Wolfe descended by elevator from the plant rooms at eleven and settled in behind his desk with beer, I repeated the press release about Cramer's return.

"Congratulations," he said. "Your handicapping skills remain strong."

"Now I suppose you want me to give you odds on whether Cramer will be calling us or dropping in."

"No, that is what gamblers would term a sure thing. It is simply a matter of when the call or visit comes. I would place my money on a visit."

"No bet. One thing is certain: any conversation with the inspector is bound to be interesting."

We had a chance to find out just how interesting after Wolfe had come down to the office at six after his visit with his orchids. No sooner had he settled in than the doorbell rang. "Wanna guess who?" I asked.

Wolfe shook his head, and I went down the hall. Through the one-way glass in the door I saw a bulky and familiar silhouette. "Good evening, sir," I said as I swung the door open for Cramer. "Welcome to Shangri-La."

"Ever the clown," he muttered. "I saw that movie way back when with Ronald Colman, and this sure ain't the place." He then went by me like an express train passing a local and headed down the hall to the office, keeping his overcoat on. It was like old times.

"So you have got your teeth into this Pierce business," Cramer was saying to Wolfe as he settled into the red leather chair and pulled out a cigar, again like old times.

"I have a client, yes, sir."

"Care to name him or her?"

"Perhaps at a later date."

"Why am I not surprised? As you know only too well, I got . . . *removed* from my position before I really got started on the Pierce business. Is it asking too much for you to fill me in on what you've learned?" he asked, chewing on the cigar, which as usual was unlit.

"Not at all sir, with this proviso," Wolfe said. "I have need of a piece of information from you."

"Whatever it is, ask and maybe I will answer—but only after I've heard what you have dug up on the murder."

"I'm afraid our catch so far is a meager one, sir," Wolfe said, "but you are welcome to what little we have." With that, he unloaded everything we had done, including my interviews with the Pierce offspring, plus Laura Cordwell and Weldon Dunagan, and Wolfe's conversation with Marchbank.

"Yeah, you sure don't have a lot," Cramer agreed when Wolfe had finished. "Any thoughts?"

"Only that I do not believe the crime syndicate was behind the killing, even though one of its own hit men almost surely was Mr. Pierce's killer," Wolfe said. "But I have a feeling you know something about that, Mr. Cramer."

"What do you mean?" the inspector barked.

"A table in the back room of a restaurant in Little Italy, where you dined not long ago with a well-known member of New York's crime syndicate."

Cramer's face almost instantly turned red. "Where in the hell did you hear about that?"

"The source is immaterial, sir. As far as I am aware, nothing about your clandestine meeting has been made public."

Cramer spat a word. "I was afraid that would come back to bite me in the butt," he said. "I figure you got this from your buddy Cohen. His paper has the best damned bloodhounds in town."

"If it is any consolation, the likelihood of the *Gazette* reporting on your conference is slim," Wolfe said. "They do not entirely trust their sources."

"I suppose as the price for keeping your mouth shut, you want to know why I sat down with Mars?"

"I do not operate in that manner, and you know it. But I would be interested in learning the rationale for your meeting with Mr. Mars."

The inspector looked like he could use a drink, but he did not ask for one. "All right, here's what happened," he said. "I got a call at home from Mars, who told me Lester Pierce was not killed under orders from what he referred to as 'the organization.'

"I then asked who did the shooting, and he said he wanted to have a face-to-face talk, that he didn't trust telephones."

"Mars probably figured you had your own line tapped," I put in.

"Maybe. Anyway, I stupidly agreed to meet him at that restaurant, which is known not only for good Italian food but also as a mob meeting place where private conversations take place."

"Hardly a prudent move on your part," Wolfe observed.

"Hell, I already said I was stupid—don't rub it in! So I went to Little Italy. There was nobody else but us in that back room, other than waiters and busboys. Mars probably had seen to that. He didn't want to be seen with me any more than I wanted to be seen with him."

"Had you previously met the man?" Wolfe asked.

"No, never. Oh, of course I had seen him on television, on news segments when he had to appear reluctantly in court over some mob troubles, so I knew what he looked like. I didn't expect to like Mars, and I was right. He's shifty, as you would expect, but at least he didn't try to feed me a line of bull.

"After we sat down, the first thing he said was, 'I know you probably don't have any use for me, and I doubt we will ever see each other again. But I want you to know what I said on the telephone: We had nothing to do with what happened to Lester Pierce. But I know who did.'

"I told him to go ahead, and he said one of his underlings— he did not give a name—was a 'loose cannon in more ways than one.' I asked what he meant, and he told me that this guy was insubordinate—that's actually the word he used. The mob apparently had employed him often as a hit man—Mars didn't say so directly, of course, though he all but admitted it. As I said, he's shifty, but he also can be transparent.

"It turns out that this hit man, whose name I didn't know at the time, had gotten into the habit of doing freelance jobs, jobs that were not 'authorized' by the syndicate. The mob doesn't mind gunning people down, as we all well know, but they like it to be their idea, and this maverick had put his so-called skill to use to make money on the side as a hired gun. Mars told me that the guy had been warned before, and now he was going to be silenced.

"'Wait a minute,' I said to him, 'give us the shooter, and we will take it from there.'

"'I can't do that,' he replied. 'We have to settle it in the family, to set an example.' I asked him if he knew who had paid his man to shoot Pierce, and he said, 'I don't know and I don't care. That's not our affair.'

"I tried to tell Mars that if the mob didn't want to be blamed for the killing, their best course would be to find out who hired the rogue gunman, but he didn't seem to give a damn. 'Hell, we'll be blamed for it anyway,' he told me."

"Did you believe Mr. Mars's version of the circumstances surrounding the Pierce shooting?" Wolfe asked.

"By and large, yes, not to say the man is trustworthy; but subsequent events have borne him out."

"Including Guido Capelli getting shot," I said.

"Yeah, as you both know, but by that time I had been put on leave," Cramer grumped.

"Was there a specific reason?" Wolfe asked.

"I had two strikes on me," the old cop said. "For one, O'Hara wanted to get rid of everyone who had been on Skinner's management team. And for two, Weldon Dunagan, who is now on the Police Review Board, hates my guts and has for years. You might remember that I once had occasion to arrest his son, and I helped put him in jail."

"I do recall that," Wolfe said. "But nevertheless, you have been returned to your old position."

"Yeah, and I'm not clear as to why that is," Cramer said, wrinkling a ruddy brow. "I do know that Rowcliff didn't exactly do a bang-up job, but I could have told them that. George is one hell of a good street dick, brave, tough, fearless, but as a manager . . . forget it. Still, I can't figure out why O'Hara brought me back. For one thing, I believe he's afraid of Dunagan and his power, and I have to wonder how the grocery store tycoon feels about me being back in harness again. He can't possibly like it. I can tell you this: all I have to do is slip up, even in a small way, and I am history," he said, making a slicing motion with his hand.

"Perhaps," Wolfe said. "In the meantime, what are your plans regarding the Pierce case?"

Cramer took a deep breath and then another. "We have got to find out who hired Capelli, and with him dead, that's not going to be a picnic."

"We tried, and with some unfortunate results," Wolfe said.

"Wait a minute," Cramer said, jerking upright. "What haven't you told me, besides the name of your client?"

Wolfe then related Saul Panzer's ill-fated attempt to learn who was behind Capelli's death, including his mugging on a Brooklyn street.

"I thought you and your men had better sense than to play games with the mob," Cramer snorted. "Panzer is lucky to be alive."

"I concur," Wolfe said. "I now have given you everything we have except our client, and I am not at liberty to divulge that information."

"I can't be concerned about that right now," the inspector replied, getting to his feet. He squinted at the cigar he had been gnawing on—he almost never lights one—and instead of hurling it at our wastebasket and missing, as is usually the case, he tucked it into the breast pocket of his suit coat and walked down the hall without a backward look.

After I had seen Cramer out and locked the front door, I returned to the office. "He definitely has mellowed," I told Wolfe.

"Manifestly. Nothing reminds a man of his mortality as much as when he is deprived of his status, especially when those doing the depriving are intellectually or morally his inferior. Clearly, Commissioner O'Hara qualifies as inferior to the inspector in the intellectual area, and although I have yet to meet Mr. Dunagan, I strongly suspect that he does not measure up morally."

"I couldn't say, although I found Dunagan to be arrogant, dismissive, and generally unpleasant during our brief meeting," I said. "Do you think Cramer suspects we—you, really—had a role in his reinstatement?"

"I do not. The inspector has consistently viewed us as adversaries, and I cannot conceive of his altering that perception. He would be shocked beyond words were he to know we had interceded on his behalf. But lest you accuse me of sentimentality," Wolfe said, "I believe it is in our best interests that he is in a position of authority within the police department. Do you choose to take issue with that stance?"

"Not in the least. This may sound strange, but I am happy—well, almost happy—to have him running the Homicide Squad again."

"But as the inspector has told us, his hold on the job remains far from secure," Wolfe cautioned. "Mr. Dunagan may prove a formidable foe. Despite all that I have heard about him, I should like to meet the man."

"What you are really saying is that you expect me to get in touch with the grocery tycoon and find a way to lure him to the brownstone for a conversation, is that what I am hearing?"

"Your hearing is most adequate."

"Assuming I can persuade him to visit you, which is a big assumption, do you have a suggested time for this meeting?"

"Tomorrow night, nine o'clock."

"Ah, I see, our daily nine p.m. chat session. This is getting to be a routine."

Wolfe's response was to open an orchid catalog and bury his nose in it. The discussion had been terminated.

CHAPTER 22

It was one thing getting Police Commissioner O'Hara to visit the brownstone. Weldon Dunagan would be quite a different matter, as I knew from meeting the man and having been summarily dismissed by him. I started the process, as I often do, by phoning Lon Cohen at the *Gazette* the next morning while Wolfe was upstairs playing with the orchids.

"Why is it that when I get a call from you, I always feel that I am about to get my pocket picked?" he said.

"What a thing for you, of all people, to say! You, who regularly help to relieve me of my hard-earned dollars at Saul Panzer's poker table. Just whose pocket is it that gets picked?"

"Can I help it if you have never learned the fine points of that noble game? Now just what sort of aid are you seeking?"

"I need to find an Achilles heel."

"Now that is a new one, I must say. Just what kind of heel are we talking about?"

"Maybe skeletons in the closet would be more accurate. We are looking for what you might have on one Weldon Dunagan."

"Ah, why do I have a feeling in my bones this has to do with the death of Lester Pierce?"

"Because you are without doubt a sensitive and perceptive member of the Fourth Estate."

"Yeah, right, Archie. What makes you believe there's anything in the way of dirt to be had on Dunagan?"

"The law of averages. The man has been obscenely rich and powerful for a long time now, and it figures that along the way, he almost certainly has been up to some sort of shenanigans, personal and/or professional, whether or not the *Gazette* has ever reported on them."

"I'm not aware of any trouble Dunagan has ever been in, but that doesn't mean it hasn't happened. I'll do some nosing around at this end. By the way, what's in it for me?"

"After all the scoops we have given the *Gazette* over the years, do you dare to even ask?"

"Oh, I dare ask, all right. You may have given us a lot of scoops, but we have fed you all manner of information that helped get us those scoops and helped Wolfe have a nice bunch of paydays."

"So it is quid pro quo, as my boss likes to say. That seems fair to me, and it's time you gave us a quid so we can eventually supply you with a pro quo."

"I will not try to dignify responding to that mangled bunch of your gibberish," Lon said.

"I won't ask you to, headline hunter. Just dig up some dirt on the tycoon who is known as 'America's Grocer' from Connecticut to California and everyplace in between. And we need it quickly."

"But of course you do. Never mind the million-plus readers who eagerly await our next information-packed edition. If we come up with what you and your boss want, can you guarantee us an exclusive on how you will use the sins and transgressions of Weldon Dunagan against him?"

"That is beyond my limited power to promise. For such a guarantee, you need to speak to Mr. Wolfe."

"Uh-huh, the old pass-the-buck trick. Or in some quarters, it's referred to as 'bait and switch.'"

"You have lost me there, but then I'm just an earnest, hard-working, underpaid private flatfoot."

"I couldn't have described you better myself," Lon said, "although I might question the 'hardworking' part."

"Very funny, and typical of your so-called sense of humor. When can we expect to hear from you?"

"Don't push it, underpaid private flatfoot. I promise I will sic one of my men on it as soon as I hang up, which I am about to do."

I was doubtful Lon's bloodhounds would dredge up any-thing about Dunagan. After all, there had been no whispers of scandal in all his time in the public light, dating from when he opened his first natural-foods grocery store in Fresno, California, twenty-five or more years ago. Since then his phiz has graced the covers of *Fortune*, *Forbes*, and even *Time*, and he once sat in on a presidential council of business advisers. It was enough to make any man arrogant, as he surely was, based on my brief meeting with him.

Imagine my surprise when, an hour later, I got a call from Lon. "Well," he said, "I really didn't think anything would turn up, but . . . it did."

"Don't keep me in suspense."

"I wouldn't dare do that. We've got an old-timer who's been here forever, named Ben Beazley, and he's got a mind like a steel trap. He doesn't do reporting anymore, he's too old and can't move around well, but we still use him on the rewrite desk, where he takes reporters' calls from out on the street and puts their dictated words into English. He's damned good at that.

"Anyway, he's got something like total recall, and he remembers an event from years back, early in Dunagan's career. We never ran a story on this, and I don't know why, but Beazley remembers a wire service piece about how Dunagan drove a small-time grocer by the name of Sunderland out of business in a little burg in Minnesota. Like he has so often over the years, Dunagan knocked out this guy's operation by slashing the prices in his own new store in town, and then once he had a monopoly, he jacked his own prices back up."

"Yeah, I have read about that tactic of his, and possibly in your very own newspaper."

"And just to cap it off, about a dozen years later, Dunagan closed the store in that hamlet because it wasn't showing a large enough profit. Now the residents have to drive fifteen miles to the nearest grocer."

"Another example of Dunagan's operating principles, or so I've read. Capitalism at work."

"But there's more," Lon said. "Sunderland committed suicide just weeks after his store folded, and then within a few months, his daughter, who was single and had been his only employee, also shot herself."

"Did the story get much exposure?"

"Only locally, not even in the Twin Cities' papers, according to Beazley. He said he took it to the *Gazette*'s wire editor at the time, but he wasn't interested. When this happened, we were in a big push to concentrate more heavily on local news. The story never got far enough up the line here that I even knew about it. I'm hearing this for the first time."

"And I suppose you're going to tell me Dunagan came out of the whole business unscathed."

"Even back then, he had a very efficient public relations machine that went to great lengths to defend the grocery chain's policies. Case in point: A psychiatrist from Minneapolis magically appeared at Sunderland's inquest, claiming that the grocer had been a patient. He testified that Sunderland had suffered from severe depression ever since his wife's death five years earlier. During the inquest, no mention was ever made of the store's closure."

"And the daughter?"

"At the inquest into her suicide, the same shrink—claiming she had also been his patient—said that for years the woman had suffered from schizophrenia. After her death, the town's small weekly paper did a somewhat amateurish feature head-lined 'An American Family's Tragedy.' No more was written anywhere about the Sunderlands, as far as Beazley knows."

"And of course nobody ever connected the shrink with the Dunagan operation, right?"

"I think that is a good assumption, Archie. I'm, of course, curious as to how you plan to put this information to use."

"That will be up to Mr. Wolfe," I replied. "But I thank you."

"That is all I get—thanks? Not a few tidbits that we can use in a story?"

"Not yet, but stay tuned."

After hanging up with Lon, I dialed the offices of Dunagan International and asked for Mrs. Kirby. "May I tell her who is calling?" the receptionist asked.

"Yes, it is Archie Goodwin. She will recognize the name."

"Hello, Mr. Goodwin," Carolyn Kirby said in an indifferent tone. "What can I do for you today?"

"As you know, my boss, Nero Wolfe, is continuing his investigation into the death of Lester Pierce, and he would very much like Mr. Dunagan to visit him at his home on West Thirty-Fifth Street tonight at nine o'clock."

"I will certainly pass along the invitation to Mr. Dunagan when he gets out of a meeting, but I must tell you that after your visit here, it seems unlikely that he will accept it. He was extremely upset for some time after you left."

"I am sorry to hear that, Mrs. Kirby. It was not my intent to cause trouble in your hallowed halls."

"I am sure it was not, but I feel it only fair to tell you how Mr. Dunagan probably will react."

"If you say one single word to him, it might help."

"Really?

"Yes, and that word is 'Sunderland.'"

"I have no idea what that means, Mr. Goodwin. Will he?"

"Oh, I believe so. I hope that after you speak that word to him, he may choose to call me."

"Perhaps he will . . ." she said, but without conviction.

Less than a half hour later, the phone rang in the office. "Goodwin, just what are you trying to pull?" Weldon Dunagan snapped. "Have you ever been sued?"

"Not recently. Are you suggesting something I have said or done might be actionable?"

Dunagan spewed a few words that questioned my parentage, then started in again, telling me where to go. The destination did not seem to be a pleasant one. I remained silent, as he seemed to be winding down, and I didn't want to rile him any further. Finally, he spoke again: "Just what is your boss up to, Goodwin?"

"He is investigating the murder of Mr. Pierce and wants to talk to you."

"What is all this Sunderland business?"

"You will have to ask Mr. Wolfe about that. I am simply the messenger."

Several seconds of silence followed. "All right, you already know what I think of private detectives," Dunagan said, "but I will come to your place tonight, if only to find out what Wolfe is trying to pull. What's the address?"

I gave it to him and said we would look forward to seeing him at nine. He responded by hanging up.

When Wolfe came down from the plant rooms after his morning session, he placed a raceme of purple *Miltonia*, one of my favorites, in the vase on his desk and rang for beer.

"Mr. Dunagan will be here at nine tonight," I told him.

He opened his eye wide, for him a show of emotion. "What means of persuasion did you employ?"

When I unloaded, he glared at me. "Your method was highly inappropriate."

"Is that so? Let's see, my assignment was to get Weldon Dunagan here, no matter how. You seemed totally uninterested in the process, so what was I to do except be resourceful?"

"I did not say 'no matter how,'" Wolfe snarled. "I expected you to use a certain amount of tact."

"Tact, with Dunagan? You must be joking. The man has all the finesse of a pile driver. He did not get to where he is by being tactful and gentlemanly. Sure, now that he's king of the hill, at least in the grocery world, he wants to be seen as some sort of elder statesman. But along the way, how many people has he trampled and driven out of business? How many other Sunderlands have there been that we have never heard about?"

"Are you finished with your diatribe?" Wolfe asked.

"I am."

"Good. Your defense of small businesses is admirable, and I commend you for it. However, there is little if anything to be gained by demonizing Mr. Dunagan at this point, whatever his moral failings."

"I will do my best to hide any animosity I feel toward the gentleman when he comes tonight. However, you may find that he has plenty of animosity to go around."

"I consider myself forewarned," Wolfe said, popping the cap off the first of two chilled beers Fritz had brought in and set before him.

CHAPTER 23

I continued to be in a fog as to why Wolfe was so interested in seeing Weldon Dunagan, especially after the grocery tycoon and I had had our short, less-than-pleasant conversation in his office. But then, I often have been unclear about my boss's actions over the years, and when I finally see the reasoning behind his moves, it usually becomes apparent.

Like our other recent nine o'clock callers, Dunagan was prompt, and I played doorman for him, greeting the man on the stoop as a white Rolls-Royce purred at the curb. "Please come in, Mr. Dunagan, I will take your coat."

He glared and said nothing, shucking the black cashmere overcoat and thrusting it at me. Not a good start. I led him down the hall to the office, where Wolfe was sitting at his desk reading. He opened his mouth to say something, but Dunagan beat him to it.

"All right, I'm here! I have already told your lackey that I've never had any use for private eyes, and the nature of your summons only reinforced that. What sort of cheap trick is this?"

"Please be seated, Mr. Dunagan," Wolfe said calmly. "May I offer you something to drink?"

"Don't try to butter me up, dammit. I did not come here to socialize. I came to learn just what your game is."

"My game, sir, is to find the murderer of Lester Pierce. Won't you reconsider my offer? We have a very fine cognac, said by some to be the best in the world."

That threw Dunagan off stride. "Well . . . I do happen to have a weakness for cognac. All right," he harrumphed as he eased himself into red leather chair and shot the cuffs on his white-on-white shirt. Without needing a signal from Wolfe, I went to the serving cart and poured a generous serving of Remisier into a snifter, placing it on the small table next to our guest along with the bottle.

"Before we get started, just what's all this about 'Sunderland'?" Dunagan demanded.

"I must apologize for Mr. Goodwin," Wolfe said smoothly. "I had asked him to invite you here this evening, and he sometimes gets overly zealous in carrying out my requests. He apparently had learned something about—"

"I was not involved in any way with what happened to those people!" Dunagan roared.

"It is of no matter," Wolfe responded, flipping a palm. "As I said before, we are here to discuss one issue and one issue only, the death of Lester Pierce."

"Of course, of course," Dunagan said, settling into the chair and taking a sip of Remisier. "But before we go any further, just what is your involvement in the case?"

"I have been employed by an individual to determine the identity of the killer or killers."

"And who is your client?"

"I am sorry, sir, but I am unable to divulge that information."

"The old lawyer-client confidentiality thing, is that it?" Dunagan said. "Except you are not a lawyer, are you?"

"I am not, nor do I wish to be. However, my covenant with those who engage me is every bit as binding as those between an attorney and his client or between a priest and his parishioner."

"Okay, so—my God, this is good," Dunagan said, licking his lips and holding up his snifter, peering at it. "Somebody could make a fortune by marketing this nectar. I could see it being sold nationally in my stores."

"Unfortunately, very little of what you refer to as 'this nectar' exists," Wolfe said. "There are nineteen bottles in the world—not counting the one before you—and all but four reside in my cellar."

"A tragedy."

"However, if the value of Remisier lies only in scarcity, perhaps it does not merit high praise."

"Maybe, but I like to fancy myself as something of a connoisseur of brandies, or of cognac, if you prefer, and this is far beyond anything I have ever tasted."

"Then by all means, have more. Mr. Goodwin has placed it well within your reach," Wolfe said.

Dunagan did not need encouragement and helped himself to a second serving. I felt like telling him that it goes down better if it is nursed, rather than gulped, but I held my tongue.

"So where was I?" our guest said. "Oh yes, I was about to ask about your progress in the investigation."

"It proceeds apace," Wolfe replied.

"That does not sound like progress to me. And lest I carp, the police seem to be doing no better. As I told Goodwin when he was at my office, my overall dissatisfaction with the New York

Police Department has led me to accept a seat on the Police Review Board."

"So I have heard. The police do appear to be stymied," Wolfe agreed.

"No wonder! Commissioner O'Hara had Rowcliff heading up Homicide, which I now concede was a mistake, but look at who he brought back, against my wishes. None other than Cramer!"

"Although I cannot say I know him well, Mr. Cramer always has seemed most professional and thorough," Wolfe said.

"Shows how much you know!" Dunagan replied.

"Perhaps you can edify me."

"You're damned right I can. Years back, he arrested my son, Kevin, during a minor fracas over in Long Island City and then testified against him in court. Kevin ended up serving two years, a blot on his record that can never be erased."

"What does your son do now?" Wolfe asked.

"I am proud to say he has been working for our company as marketing vice president for more than ten years."

"What was the Long Island City set-to about?"

"Ah, some petty argument over drugs," Dunagan said with a sniff, waving the offense away with a hand. "At the time, the police were cracking down on pushers, and poor Kevin got caught in the middle."

"Was he a drug user?"

"Everybody was back then, hardly a big deal."

"Let us speculate for a moment about what might have occurred had Inspector Cramer not happened on the scene," Wolfe said.

"The old 'what-might-have-been' game," Dunagan said. He shook his head and gave a laugh that held no mirth.

"Speculation to be sure, sir. But let us assume the fracas, as you call it, had continued uninterrupted. It is conceivable that one or more of the combatants might have been maimed for life or killed. Your son could have ended up either the killer or a victim."

"Could have, could have. What is the point of all this, Wolfe?"

"The point is that Inspector Cramer, the man you decry, may well have done the Dunagan family an immeasurable favor. Yes, your son did serve prison time, and yes, that without doubt carries a certain stigma. But by all accounts, he has done well in the years since his incarceration. It seems to me Mr. Cramer is owed thanks rather than damnation."

Dunagan considered Wolfe's words, his mood mellowed by the consumption of Remisier. "Are you some sort of buddy of Cramer's?"

"We know each other, but one would hardly term us friends. Do you agree, Archie?"

"Absolutely. Those two have said things to each other that . . . well, are best not repeated."

"I've always considered myself fair, Wolfe," Dunagan said, "tough but fair. Hell, I've had to be tough to survive in the dog-eat-dog business world. But I will take what you say about Cramer under advisement. Now what about Lester's killing?"

"Mr. Pierce's death is, of course, the real purpose of this meeting, sir. Do you remain convinced the crime syndicate was behind the shooting?"

"I did originally, but I have rethought my position. At first, I felt the mob had every reason to want Lester out of the way. But then on reflection, I had to concede that up to now, Three-G has simply not been effective in its war against organized crime, so what would be the mob's gain in killing Lester?"

"Your point is well taken," Wolfe said. "Also, doing away with Mr. Pierce would not eliminate the Good Government Group, would it? I am led to assume that as principal financer, you plan to continue your support of the group with someone steering the ship."

"Absolutely! I am as committed to Three-G's work as ever."

"As you now do not feel the crime syndicate was behind Mr. Pierce's murder, do you have any thoughts as to who was responsible for the killing?"

Dunagan stared into his snifter before replying. "I have given that a lot of thought, of course, and frankly I cannot imagine who would have any reason to want Lester dead."

"Are you aware of any threats that have been directed at other employees of the Good Government Group?"

"I have not been told of any, and I'm sure I would have heard had that been the case," Dunagan said. "Back to Lester's death. What does trouble me is that it sure had some characteristics of a mob hit."

"As was no doubt intended. And it is all but certain that the shooter was indeed a syndicate hit man, but one operating in this situation as a freelancer under the temporary employ of another individual."

"Who?"

"That is precisely the question I hope to answer."

"What's stopping you—or the police—from grilling the shooter if you know his identity?"

"That is impossible. He too has been shot dead, and in all probability by the syndicate itself, which does not appreciate its employees being hired by others."

"Do the police know this?" Dunagan asked.

"I am sure they are aware of the situation, given their army of investigators. So we are agreed that the syndicate was not responsible for Mr. Pierce's killing."

Dunagan laughed—actually laughed. "Give me more of this superb cognac, and I will agree to almost anything."

"The bottle remains at your disposal," Wolfe said. "If you do not object, I will pose questions you may already have been asked by Mr. Goodwin when he visited you in your office."

"Fine," Dunagan said with the carefree wave of a hand. "Ask away."

"Is it fair to say you knew Lester Pierce well?"

"Absolutely. We worked together hand in glove in shaping the Good Government Group. He shared my antipathy toward corrupt governmental practices—of which there are many—and obviously toward the crime syndicate. I could not have wanted a better partner in this venture."

"How much did you know about the man's private life?"

"As much as I needed to," Dunagan said. "Although we did not socialize a great deal, I had met Audra several times, and I was impressed by her commitment to a variety of fine causes. I also met each of their children, and they all seemed solid."

"Were you aware of any extramarital relations Mr. Pierce had?"

"I was not, and I find it hard to believe there were any. Good heavens, the man was a pillar of his church. Now I am not a very religious person myself, Mr. Wolfe"—he had now added a "Mr." in addressing my boss, so the Remisier was working its magic—"but I respect and admire those who are. How, I ask you, could someone so devout behave in such a way?"

"Outward piety is hardly a guarantee of inward virtues," Wolfe said. "Jesus of Nazareth made that clear to his followers with these words: 'When you pray, do not be like the hypocrites, for they love to pray standing on the street corners to be seen by men. . . . When you pray, go into your room, close the door and pray to your Father, who is unseen. Then your Father, who sees what is done in secret, will reward you.'"

"I am impressed by your biblical knowledge," Dunagan said with a nod.

"Do not be; the Bible is literature," Wolfe replied, "and several of its translations warrant a place in any good library."

"I still find it very difficult to believe that Lester would have broken his wedding vows."

"There has been speculation to the contrary," Wolfe said. "I do not make it a habit to trade in gossip, but you should know that Mr. Pierce apparently had a liaison with another member of the organization's staff."

"Which would be Laura Cordwell!" Dunagan barked, jerking upright. "Dammit, when she got hired, I had to wonder if her good looks might have had something to do with her getting the position—and whether her presence would become a distraction."

"From what I have been told, however, she has been most capable at her job," Wolfe remarked.

"That's what Lester always told me, but if she . . . if he . . ." Dunagan drew in air and seemed to run down like an alarm clock whose jangling was ignored.

"As I said, sir, we are in the realm of speculation regarding Miss Cordwell, and we shall move on," Wolfe said. "To your knowledge, had Mr. Pierce ever been threatened by anyone?"

"If he had, I never knew about it," Dunagan said, shaking his head vigorously. "I cannot think of a soul. He was an extremely likable man, gregarious, friendly, and generous."

"Would you say he was universally liked within the Good Government Group?"

"It always seemed that way to me. I often sat in on the staff meetings that Lester chaired, and it was clear that he was admired by all of them."

"Admiration is not necessarily synonymous with likability."

"You sure are a stickler with words, aren't you? All right then, it seemed to me he was both admired *and* liked."

"Might the fact you were present have affected the way members of the group acted toward Mr. Pierce?"

"I really don't think so. I attended these sessions often enough that everyone was used to my presence in the room. And I rarely spoke up. My method of operation is to hire good people and then leave them alone to do their jobs."

"A good policy," Wolfe said. "How would you describe Mr. Pierce's management style?"

"It was similar to my own, which may explain why we got along so well. He too tried to find good people and let them do their work without interference from above. Like me with my company, he did not micromanage, which seems to be a hot new business term."

"Did you approve of all those he hired?"

"Well . . . I mentioned earlier my reservation about Laura, but then she turned out to be energetic and full of ideas about how to make Three-G more relevant and more effective. Now, after what you have told me about her, I really don't know what to think.

"Lester also hired Roland Marchbank," Dunagan continued. "In fact, that was his very first hire, even before Laura. He jumped into his job as assistant executive director with great enthusiasm. My reservation about Roland is that he tends toward being overly confrontational, and he does not take criticism from other staffers well. However, I still believe that he will be a fine executive director.

"As to other hires, most of them have been eager recent college graduates who have a burning desire to change the world. One local newspaper referred to these young men and women as 'Pierce's Pride of Lions' for their tenacity and their high-minded crusading against governmental corruption. Because of the work of some of these young people, two members of the city council were removed from their seats for bribery and graft, and one building department head was indicted for pocketing city funds. Now I don't mean to say these kids did all the work in these cases, not at all, but they really dug into records and files, real bulldogs they were, and tireless."

"I have read about these young people in newspaper articles," Wolfe said. "Will they work as well with Mr. Marchbank as they did with his predecessor?"

"I honestly believe so, despite how worshipful they were toward Lester. Some of them thought of him as almost godlike."

"You already have stated you don't believe anyone within the Good Government Group was responsible for Mr. Pierce's death. Surely, however, it is possible that he made enemies elsewhere because of the investigative nature of the organization's work."

"Of course he—and Three-G—did make their share of enemies; that comes with the territory," Dunagan said. "We stepped on a lot of toes over the years and got a few people tossed out of their jobs, and deservedly so. But having said that, I cannot think of anyone angry enough, or desperate enough, to want to kill Lester."

"Very well. If upon reflection an individual occurs to you, please inform Mr. Goodwin. Now if you will excuse me, I bid you a good evening," Wolfe said, rising and walking out of the office.

"That was certainly an abrupt exit," Dunagan said, turning to me with a puzzled expression.

"Mr. Wolfe is like that," I said. "Don't take offense. He wastes no time on small talk, and when his business is concluded, he sometimes behaves in a brusque manner."

"I'll say it's brusque. Oh, well, the evening was not a complete waste," Dunagan said, eyeing his empty snifter. "That cognac alone was worth the visit. As I said before, it is tragic that so little of it exists."

CHAPTER 24

After I watched Weldon Dunagan go down the front steps of the brownstone and ease into the backseat of his chauffeured Rolls-Royce, I returned to the office to find Wolfe behind his desk again, nose in a book.

"Mr. Dunagan was somewhat taken aback by your abrupt departure from the room," I said, getting a glare in response. "Of course, I was a little fazed myself by what you said to him: 'We are here to discuss one matter and one matter only, the murder of Lester Pierce.' You almost had me fooled by that."

Wolfe set his book down and glared again but said nothing. "The sole purpose of your inviting Dunagan here tonight was to change his attitude toward Inspector Cramer, isn't that so, Chief?" He hates it when I call him "chief" even more than when I call him "boss."

"Are you quite through?" Wolfe said icily.

"I am. I do think you were successful, though, regarding the inspector, so I suppose it is fair to say that something got accomplished tonight. But just where do we go from here?"

"I suggest you go to bed, which is what I plan to do after I have finished this chapter. We will discuss the matter in the morning."

I did not know if he said that just to put me off, or whether he really meant it, but the next morning, when he came down to the office from visiting his "concubines," as he likes to refer to the orchids, I swiveled to face him. "Well?"

"Well, what?" he demanded as he pressed the buzzer under his desk drawer, signaling Fritz to bring in beer.

"Well, we have something to discuss, or have you forgotten?"

"I never forget anything. I have been thinking about an assignment, and you may not like it."

"Try me."

"The syndicate gunman, who was himself shot, Guido Capelli, must have some next of kin. I suggest you find them and learn everything you can about him. Knowing what befell Saul, I do not propose this mission lightly."

"Assuming Capelli is the one who shot Pierce, which I believe to be true, what you really want to know is who hired him."

"And I realize that may not be possible," Wolfe said.

"But we might be able to find out something about him that will help us. It's a lot better than sitting on our collective hands. I know just where to start."

If that last bit sounded boastful, it really wasn't. My starting point was only a few feet from my desk—the shelves where we keep copies of the last two weeks of issues of the *Times* and *Gazette*. Knowing the date on which Capelli had been shot, I went first to the *Times*, which generally has a longer list of death notices. Sure enough, it jumped out at me:

CAPELLI—Guido L.

of Brooklyn, passed away at the age of 37, on November 17, loving son of Maria, cherished brother of Marcantonio and Cecilia.

Services and burial were private.

This was a start. I went to the Brooklyn telephone directory and, wonder of wonders, found two Capellis in the book, Cecilia and Marcantonio. There was no listing for Guido. I then called Lon, who answered as usual with a gruff "Cohen, what is it?"

"You really need to work on your telephone manners," I said. "I need a favor, a small one."

"Never mind my telephone manners—I'm a busy man, unlike you. You always refer to your favors as small, no matter how much time and trouble they end up causing," he said.

"Now you know that simply is not true. Besides, many of those favors eventually come back to you in the form of exclusive stories."

A grunt for effect came through the wire. "All right, what is it this time? Spit it out."

"I would like to know what, if anything, you have in your files on one Marcantonio Capelli."

"Now just why does that surname sound so familiar?" Lon asked. "Might this Marcantonio be a relative of a certain gentleman—and I use that term loosely—who made news recently by getting himself shot, and very possibly by the very same group of people whom he had toiled for?"

"You are most perceptive, which may be why you now hold an exalted position at what has been called the fifth-largest daily newspaper in all of America."

"What d'ya mean, *called*? It *is* the fifth-largest paper in all the land, and not far behind number four, either."

"Okay, enough of your breast-beating. I bow to the honored position of your publication. Now, can you or one of your many underlings see if you have written anything about this Marcantonio?"

Lon told me that, as busy as the staff was, he would find someone to scour the paper's morgue. Sure enough, less than half an hour later, he telephoned.

"Here is what we've got on your not-so-good boy: Six years ago, Marcantonio Capelli was arrested for armed robbery. He held up a deli in Brooklyn, and the owner called the police seconds after he had left the store. He was nabbed three blocks away with the cash in his pocket. He got two years but was paroled after serving half the time. Four years ago, Capelli was caught again, in the act of holding up a Queens filling station when its owner triggered an alarm tied to a police station while our Mr. C. was still in the place. He got only a year because when he was caught, he didn't have a weapon."

"Hardly a high-wattage lightbulb, is he? Anything else?"

"That's it," Lon said.

"What's his age?"

"Let's see, he was twenty-eight six years ago. My high school math tells me that would make him thirty-four now."

"You got any idea what he does for a living?"

"No, but I hope robbery isn't full-time work, because he sure as hell hasn't been very good at that. I assume you want to talk to him about his brother."

"Now there's a good assumption."

"Well, be careful. He may not take kindly to being quizzed."

"Believe it or not, that has occurred to me."

"Just remember where you got the information and what a good friend I am."

"I will be sure to file that away for future reference."

After hanging up, I turned to Wolfe. "I am going to pay a visit to the late Guido Capelli's brother, Marcantonio, in Brooklyn, assuming I can find him at home, and see what, if anything, I can learn about the recently deceased. The younger sibling seems to have gone astray as well, according to the *Gazette*'s files."

"I trust you will be armed."

"I will," I told him, opening the safe and pulling out the shoulder holster, strapping it on, slipping my trusty Marley .32 into it, and sliding a silencer, which I call a "tongue loosener," into my coat pocket.

"Do not do anything reckless," Wolfe said as I rose to leave.

"Reckless, me? I have grown too fond of myself over the years to place yours truly in harm's way."

Wolfe scowled, returning to his book, and I left, walking over to Curran Motors and picking up the Heron sedan. Traffic was light, so I got over to Brooklyn in twenty minutes. I had no trouble finding the address on a modest, tree-lined street in Bushwick. The two-story brick building that butted up to the sidewalk looked like a smaller and more tired version of Wolfe's brownstone.

Apparently, this was a single-family residence, because the only buzzer next to the front door had a card with CAPELLI on it. I pushed and waited. Nothing. I pushed again, several times.

"Yeah, what is it?" a voice squawked.

"Marcantonio?" I spoke into the intercom.

"Yeah, what?"

"I need to see you about your brother."

He answered with an obscenity. I leaned into the buzzer again and held it down.

"Awright, awright, dammit, I'm coming down. Don't have a conniption."

I stood on the stoop for a full minute. Finally, the door opened, and a short, dark guy with a ducktail hairstyle and wearing a black, zippered jacket came out and peered at me, blinking his eyes as if they were unused to sunlight. "Whaddya want?" he demanded.

"I'd like to talk to you about your brother."

"Why?"

"We're looking into why he got shot."

"Who's *we*?" he said, giving me what I'm sure he thought was a tough-guy sneer. He looked like he was central casting's idea of one of the gang members in *West Side Story*.

"Private cops," I said.

"Let's go where we can talk privatelike," he said. "My mama, she's upstairs sleeping. I don't wanna disturb her. Follow me."

We walked down the block until we came to an alley, something you don't see in Manhattan. "Let's go in here and talk," Capelli said. "I don't wanna to be seen with no cop, private or otherwise." We stepped into the alley that had a dogleg, which meant part of it was hidden from the street.

I did not like being in an enclosed area, remembering what happened to Saul recently in a gangway, and my instincts were a couple of seconds slow. Capelli's fist caught me on the left cheekbone, and I staggered back as he got ready to throw a second punch.

But now he was the one to be slow. I was ready for him and drove my own fist into his gut, which was flabbier than I thought, given his lean build. He doubled over with a moan and started to retch as I drove a left to his chin, which felled him. When he tried to get up, I whipped out the Marley.

"Stay right there, Hotspur," I barked. It turned out he wasn't any better as a fighter than as a robber. "Now that really wasn't very nice. And here I thought we were going to have a friendly chat."

"You son of a bitch," he muttered, still lying on his back.

"Not a very smart way to talk to someone who's looking down a gun barrel at you," I said. "Who killed your brother?"

"Who do you think, wise guy?"

"Not sure, which is why I'm asking. No, don't try to get up. You're fine down there. Now, let's start again," I said, keeping my Marley pointed at him. "Tell me who you think killed Guido."

He looked up at me and smirked, as if to say, *What are you going to do, shoot me right here and have people from all up and down the block come running to see what happened?*

I reached into my pocket and pulled out an item that changed his expression instantly—the silencer. I calmly fitted it to the Marley, repeating the question and keeping the weapon pointed at him. His one line of defense against me was now gone, although what he didn't realize was that I would never shoot him, silencer or not.

"Hey, come on, will ya?" he said in a hoarse tone, eyes suddenly wide open and drool coming out of his mouth. "You know what happened to Guido."

"I would like to hear it from you."

"They got him, the . . . the boys, you know?"

"The organization?"

"Yeah, right. Now please put your roscoe down."

"Maybe later. Now why did they kill him? Wasn't he a loyal employee?"

"I . . . I . . ."

"Speak up! I can't hear you, and I'm beginning to feel kind of twitchy," I said, jabbing the Marley at him and pretending to have the shakes.

"Guido, he . . . sometimes . . . did jobs they didn't like, you know?"

"No, I don't know. Tell me about it."

"He, well, he took what you might call . . . *outside* contracts, you know what I mean?"

"You mean jobs for other people, and people who were not part of the organization?"

He nodded as tears started forming in his eyes. He really thought he was a dead man, and I was not about to disabuse him of that.

"Who hired your brother that last time, the time just before he got himself killed?"

"I don't know," Marcantonio said as he began to sob. "It was somebody rich and lived good, I think, but he never said a name."

"Was it a man or a woman?"

"I don't know, Mister, honest I don't even know that. Guido didn't never tell me much about what he was doing. 'It's not healthy for you to know,' that's what he said to me."

"So, nothing he said to you about that last job gave you any idea who was hiring him, is that what you're telling me?" I said, waving the Marley around again in what was meant to be a reckless gesture.

"Yes, sir. Just that this . . . person had already paid him part of what he would get once the . . ."

"Once the job was over," I finished his sentence. "When was he going to get the rest, and where would he get it?"

"Someplace in Manhattan, I think. But as I said before, Guido didn't like to talk at all about what he did."

"Did he do a lot of these outside jobs?"

"Yeah, I think so, although I didn't ever know, not even once, who he was working for."

"Did you live together?"

He nodded. "Him and me and Mama, we were all together. Guido wanted the telephone to be in my name. He liked to be real private, you know?"

"But he wasn't all that private because people knew how to get hold of him so they could hire him. What about your sister, Cecilia, isn't it?"

He seemed surprised at how much I knew. "She lives over in Prospect Heights in her own flat, but I'm pretty sure she don't know nothing about what Guido was doing. Don't bother her, she's a real good kid."

"Let's talk about you now, Marcantonio. Just what is it you do to support yourself?"

"I work on the docks, day labor. I show up every morning and they hand out the jobs."

"Do you usually get work that way?"

"Most days, yeah, if I'm there early enough; it's a living. What else am I gonna do?"

"After Guido got killed, what happened to the money he already was paid for the hit?"

He frowned and tried to look puzzled. "I guess maybe he spent it."

"I guess maybe he didn't have time to spend it," I said. "I think that you have it."

"You shaking me down?" he whined. "That ain't fair. I need that dough for Mama. She got left with nothin' for herself when Papa died after all his years working on the docks."

"But your mama had three kids. Don't all of you take care of her and make sure she has enough to live on?"

That threw Marcantonio, and before he could mount a comeback, I prodded him to stand up. "Let's go to your place right now," I said, gesturing with the pistol. "I want to see the money Guido got."

The younger Capelli brother looked like he was going to start crying again, but he got to his feet slowly as I slipped the Marley into my jacket and kept my hand on it. As we walked the half block to his house, he kept looking around as if to find help. But there wasn't any on the all-but-deserted street.

When we climbed the steps, he drew the keys out of his pocket and opened the front door. I was right behind him as we entered. The living room was on the right, a dark, heavily curtained room with bulky furniture that looked like it belonged in the previous century except for the small television with a rabbit-ears aerial that sat on a folding metal table in one corner.

"The money's in my room," Marcantonio whispered. "I don't want to wake Mama. Since what happened to Guido, she sleeps most of the time." He started up the stairs with me at his heels.

"I'll go up alone," he said over his shoulder.

"No, you won't," I countered in a whisper, jabbing him with the revolver. There were several doors along the wallpapered second-floor hallway, one of which was ajar. A faint, questioning voice came from within, words I couldn't make out.

"It's all right, Mama. I got a friend with me. Go back to sleep," her son said, closing her door. We entered another bedroom, with a window that looked out into a drab and grassless backyard. Marcantonio went to a bureau, pulling open a drawer and reaching in under a pile of clothes. He came out with a shoebox, which he reluctantly handed to me.

I took the lid off and looked at stacks of used currency, twenties and fifties, which filled the box to the top. "How much is in here?" I asked.

"A grand. Guido was supposed to get another thou after he did the job, but . . . you know what happened."

"Yeah. Who gave him this?"

"I dunno know, honest I don't. He just said he had a live one, like I told you, a rich one. Wouldn't tell me a thing, but he was like that. He never said who his jobs was for."

"You have any idea where this . . . *client* lived?"

He shook his head. "Naw, I'm tellin' ya, he didn't never talk about his work, either for the outfit or when he was doing them jobs on the side."

"How did your mama think Guido earned a living?"

"He told her he was in sales and that seemed to be okay with her. You gotta remember that she's old and don't speak hardly any English," he said, nodding toward her closed door. "I really need that money to take care of her," he added in a whiny voice.

"Take it," I said, holding the box out to him. "I don't want it. But now that I know where you live, I might be visiting you again to see if you remember anything more about who Guido did that job for."

Marcantonio gave what I'm sure was a sigh of relief as I turned and went down the stairs and out the front door. I hoped I had seen the last of the tired old house in Bushwick.

CHAPTER 25

I got back to the brownstone just in time for lunch, but I did not report to Wolfe then because of course any talk of business is verboten during meals. In the office with coffee later, Wolfe remarked about the bruise on my left cheek. "Perhaps you fell?"

"Perhaps I did not, but to resurrect an oft-used boxing quote, 'You shoulda seen the other guy!' Would you like a report?" He nodded.

I proceeded to describe my visit to Brooklyn, leaving nothing out. When I finished, I said, "It seems I haven't brought back a lot to show for my time."

"We know a little more than when we—" Wolfe was interrupted by the telephone. I picked up my receiver and gave my usual greeting.

"Mr. Goodwin, this is Audra Pierce. I would like to speak to Nero Wolfe, if he is available."

I cupped the receiver and identified our caller to Wolfe, who picked up his phone while I stayed on the line.

"Madam, I have nothing more to report at present," he told our caller.

"But I have something to report to you," she said. "I was visited by Inspector Cramer today, and he just left. I must say he is both brighter and more civil than Captain Rowcliff, which makes me wonder why Lester did not like him. He was quite thorough in his questioning—and polite as well."

"That does not surprise me, madam."

"What might surprise you, though, is that he asked about you."

"To what end?"

"To be specific, he asked me if I knew you and I am afraid he caught me off guard, as I was a little slow in responding. I finally said to him, 'Why are you asking?' and he said, 'Just curious.' I then told him that I had heard of you, of course, but that I hadn't met you. However, because of the way he looked at me, I am pretty sure he felt I was lying. I am sorry."

"There is nothing to be sorry about," Wolfe replied. "Does it concern you that the inspector may think you have hired me?"

"No, it really does not."

"It does not disquiet me, either. I suspect I will be hearing from Mr. Cramer before long."

"Oh, dear, I hope that I have not caused a problem for you."

"Not at all, I am used to visits from Mr. Cramer. During your meeting, did he tell you anything you found to be of interest?"

"Not really. He obviously wanted to know if Lester had any enemies, anyone who disliked him enough to kill him, and I am afraid I was not much help to him, as I haven't been to you as well. I am sorry to hear you have no news, but I will remain optimistic."

Wolfe said good-bye and I stayed on the line, assuring her that we would telephone her when we had something to report.

"Well, do you want to bet on how long before Cramer comes calling?" I asked Wolfe.

"No, but I would be surprised if we do not hear from him, either in person or by telephone, before I go up to visit the orchids at four."

Sure enough, a few minutes before three, the doorbell rang. "There he is, right on schedule!" I told Wolfe.

"Nice to see you again," I told Cramer as I opened the front door.

"I'm not sure that I can say the same," the inspector growled as he stepped in and headed down the hall to the office, with me in his wake as usual.

"Good afternoon, sir," Wolfe said, looking up from a book.

"I have yet to see one single thing that's good about it," Cramer responded, dropping into the red leather chair that he has occupied so often that he seems to own it. "I just came from a visit with Audra Kingston Pierce, who is quite the lady," he said, jamming the unlit cigar into his mouth.

"So I have been told."

"As you say. Is she your client?"

"Yes, she is," Wolfe said.

"I thought so! On a hunch, I asked her if she knew you, and she paused before answering, then told me she had heard of you but hadn't met you. Mrs. Pierce is an attractive and cultured lady, but she is a poor liar."

"Liar is too strong a word," Wolfe replied. "I prefer to say she was being evasive."

"Have it your way. In any event, she was not at all forthcoming about her relationship with you."

"Perhaps she felt I would prefer that our arrangement remain private. Did you learn anything helpful from her?"

"Not really. She told me she and Pierce had not been close in recent years, and while she did not come right out and say that he had a roving eye, she certainly suggested it."

"What is your next step?" Wolfe asked.

Cramer snorted. "Look, I know I am following in your tracks here, or at least in Goodwin's. I also have Rowcliff's notes from when he talked to them all, and I didn't learn much, but then George has never been a very good interviewer. That's off the record, of course. Got any advice for me?"

"I do not, sir, except to say this: when you have completed your interviews with them, I suggest we meet and compare notes."

"Do you now? That is not something I'm used to hearing from you. This case is important to me, Wolfe, and I don't want to be fed a line of gobbledy-gook here."

"I am quite serious about our working together, Mr. Cramer. And in all candor, it is in my interest that you get whatever credit is due in this matter."

That brought a guffaw from the inspector. "Now I get it," he said, clapping his beefy hands twice. "Whatever our past skirmishes, you would rather deal with me than with someone like Rowcliff or even, heaven forbid, our current excuse for a commissioner, who would love nothing more than to present me with my walking papers."

"I am not about to argue that point, sir. Will you have something to drink? It is to my shame as a host that I did not offer you a libation earlier. I am about to have beer."

"Well, I am on duty but—what the hell, I'll have one, too. The nice thing about being an inspector—and I still am one, at least for the time being—is that I have a driver, and during working hours, he has to be cold sober. It wouldn't look good if the driver of a police vehicle got a DWI."

While I listened, the two of them reviewed the career of Lester Pierce. "I only met him a couple of times," Cramer said, "but I found him to be a grade-A stuffed shirt, or maybe a cold fish is a better description.

"He had this superior attitude, saying—in a patronizing way—that he held the greatest respect for the police department, but that he felt it was in desperate need of new blood, preferably college trained, and of embracing what he referred to as 'the new realities of urban law enforcement in these postmodern times,' whatever the hell that means."

"I never met Mr. Pierce, but I understand he was possessed of political ambitions," Wolfe said.

Cramer took a sip of his beer. "As the story goes, he badly wanted to be governor, and he was using his job as head of Three-G to burnish his reputation as a civic reformer."

"What have you learned about his character?"

"I know exactly where you're going with this," Cramer said. "As his wife alluded to, the man was a skirt chaser, a discreet one, of course. But discretion or not, word has a way of getting out. The fact is that we all, every one of us, end up paying for our sins."

"You are being philosophical today," Wolfe said.

"Maybe. After all, look who ended up dining with a Mafia boss, and not so long ago."

"But you did not get caught in the act," I said.

"Not yet, anyway, although I've gotten wind of rumors about that evening that are floating around."

"Back to Mr. Pierce," Wolfe said. "What have you learned about his alleged liaisons?"

"You are asking every question this afternoon," Cramer replied sharply. "It's all take and no give."

"Very well, sir. What do you wish to know?"

"Talk to me about what you have learned concerning Lester Pierce's extracurricular activities."

Wolfe turned to me, preferring to avoid the subject. "He is said to have had an extremely close relationship with one of his employees, the very attractive former beauty queen, Laura Cordwell," I said.

"So I have heard," the inspector replied. "You've talked to her, Goodwin. What does she have to say for herself?"

"I did sit down with her in her office at Three-G all right, face-to-face, and when I brought up the question of her personal relationship with Pierce, she figuratively slammed the door on me. End of story. On that particular subject, my advice would be to approach the lady with caution."

"I will take that into consideration," Cramer said in a tone that indicated he was not looking forward to meeting with the woman.

"When I get done talking to her, and all the others, I will get back to you," he said, rising and walking out of the office. "And by the way, thanks for the beer; I needed it."

CHAPTER 26

For several days, the murder of Lester Pierce was all but forgotten in the brownstone and also in the pages of the city's newspapers. Wolfe toiled for hours writing yet another article for one of the orchid publications he subscribes to, and I found myself happily spending a lot of time with Lily, dancing with her at the Churchill, dining at Rusterman's Restaurant, and going to the Garden to see the Rangers wallop Toronto.

I kept hoping Wolfe would suddenly close his eyes and that his lips would begin to push out and in, out and in, which is what occurs when he plays at being a genius and solves a case. No such luck.

On a Wednesday morning when I was in the office typing up Wolfe's magazine article, the phone rang. Never was I so happy to hear Inspector Cramer's voice.

"I have talked to all those people, and I want to sit down with Wolfe and go over what I came up with. I have an inkling about Pierce's killer, a strong inkling."

I've got a lot of respect for Inspector Cramer—along with some reservations. I never thought he wasn't smart, but his kinds of smarts are in no way similar to Wolfe's kinds. Cramer tends to be a plodder, albeit a tenacious one, while Wolfe possesses flashes of inspiration, flashes he cannot even describe. "I have genius or nothing," he has said in defining himself.

So when Cramer tells me he has "an inkling," I take it with the proverbial grain of salt. Usually, he is so far behind Wolfe that when the murderer is unmasked, it comes as a surprise to the inspector. As I was to learn, though, things would be different this time around.

But we were not at the end of the story just yet. I told Cramer that I would have Wolfe call him to set up a meeting. Only seconds after I hung up, the phone rang. It was Lon Cohen.

"Archie, you are not going to like this news," he said. "I'm really sorry to be its bearer."

"Well, hit me with it."

"I know that you don't read one of our afternoon competitors, the *Journal-American*. They have a columnist named Everett who writes a feature called Just Between Us, which is a poor imitation of Chad Preston's East Side, West Side, All Around the Town, with which you are familiar."

"Okay, so?"

"So, we just got a copy of their first edition, and here is what Mr. Everett leads his column with:

> We have it on good authority that the reinstated Homicide Squad boss Inspector L. T. Cramer was seen dining recently with mob kingpin Ralph Mars in the back room of a well-known Mafia eatery down in Little Italy. The subject of their conversation is not known, but the meeting has everyone abuzz at Police Headquarters on Centre

Street. We have as of deadline time been unable to get any comment, either from Cramer or his bosses.

"I'll be damned."

"Me too, Archie, particularly because neither Chad Preston nor anyone else at the *Gazette* will run an item without either an attribution or some sort of confirmation. Therein lies the reason we never published an item about the Little Italy meeting."

"You've got higher standards," I said.

"True, and sometimes we end up paying for those standards, not that I am complaining. I take some comfort in the fact that our circulation is considerably larger than the *Journal-American's*."

"What's your next move?"

"First, to find out who leaked that item to Everett. Next, to get a quote from Cramer and to learn what the higher-ups at headquarters think about this item. I have already put Preston on it, and he says he has a hunch."

"Care to share it?"

"Why not? He thinks Rowcliff is the leak."

"That would hardly be surprising, given that he lusted after the top spot in Homicide and instead, he's been kicked sideways, or maybe even down one flight of stairs."

"I would say down is the correct direction, Archie. As respected as the Traffic Department may be, this is definitely not where Rowcliff wants to spend the rest of his career. I've already heard about his grumbling from Chad Preston, who says he's been going around the building moaning about how unfairly he's been treated. And Chad says that it is common knowledge at 240 Centre Street that he, Rowcliff, feels Cramer never really valued him, so there may be some bad blood in the works here."

"There's absolutely no question as to which of those two is the classier—or the more able."

"Yeah, but as you are aware, class and ability do not necessarily rise to the top," Lon said.

"Agreed. Please keep us posted on developments. This is not going to make my boss happy."

"Nor should it. I would still like to know exactly what that conversation between Cramer and Mars was all about. Apparently, Everett at the *Journal-American* doesn't know either, or he would have written about it. Anyway, Archie, as I said, I am going to turn Chad Preston loose on this whole business and see what he comes up with."

"I'll be interested in hearing what shakes out," I told Lon, neglecting of course to mention that Wolfe and I already knew the essence of the Cramer-Mars tête-à-tête. So it seemed that the inspector was back in the soup once again. I recalled what he had said last time he was here about "paying for our sins."

When Wolfe came down from the plant rooms, I filled him in on the latest developments, and he rewarded me with a glower.

"Okay, I am not happy about this, either," I told him. "What do you think about Cramer saying he has an inkling as to who Pierce's killer is?"

"Pfui. I am not about to quibble over Mr. Cramer's use of *inkling*, which the dictionary defines as 'a slight knowledge or vague notion.' I suspect what the inspector really means is that he has a strong idea as to who the guilty party is. But then, so do I, although he and I may not be in agreement."

"Care to share a name with me?"

"Not at present. I am still working my way through the mare's nest created by Mr. Rowcliff and that *Journal-American* knave."

"Do you think this latest business has the potential of sinking Cramer's ship for good?"

"Possibly, although I am optimistic that Mr. Cohen and the *Gazette*'s highly competitive columnist Preston still have arrows in their quiver that may prove effective in foiling the attack upon Mr. Cramer."

"I hope you are right, although that stuff running in the *J-A* seems awfully damning and needs some sort of response."

"I have a feeling, Archie, that at least a portion of the response you desire may come from a surprising quarter," Wolfe said.

I tried to question Wolfe as to what he meant, but he would say nothing more, instead busying himself with signing the stack of correspondence from other orchid fanciers that I had typed up earlier. It was not until after lunch—at 3:10 to be precise—that we got word of another development, which came in the form of a telephone call from—who else?—Lon Cohen.

"Is Mr. Wolfe on the line with you?" he asked, and I signaled Wolfe to pick up.

"He is now."

"Okay, this Chad Preston column will run in our final edition today, which has not yet been delivered to you. Here it is:

> *The source behind the unconfirmed rumor in another publication that Inspector Lionel T. Cramer had been seen dining with syndicate biggie Ralph Mars is none other than Captain George Rowcliff. Rowcliff recently got bumped from his spot as acting head of the Homicide Squad by Cramer, who returned to his old post. Attempts to reach both men for comment had been unsuccessful by press time, but we will continue our efforts to talk to them.*

"Now what do you think of that?" Lon asked.

"Has there been any reaction yet from either Commissioner O'Hara or Weldon Dunagan?" Wolfe asked.

"No, but I would not be surprised if Chad is on the horn to one or both of them as we speak. Then things should get even more interesting."

"The glee is apparent in your voice," I said.

"Not glee, Archie, but certainly the competitive juices are flowing," Lon said. "This Everett has been trying to run Cramer down mainly because Preston's columns have defended the inspector. That's what happens when a guy is number two in the column game, and Everett is definitely number two, a distant second."

"I know you will update us with bulletins as they occur," I told him. "Don't be shy about calling."

"Shy—me? Not a chance."

CHAPTER 27

We had barely gotten settled in the office with coffee when the telephone rang. "That will be Lon," I told Wolfe, and I was right.

"Seems like all I'm doing lately is reading to you, and now I'm about to do it again," he said as I motioned to Wolfe to pick up his phone.

"Well, let the record show that we here in the brownstone appreciate it," I said. "Are we going to like what you've got for us?"

"Oh, I believe you will," Lon replied. "This is not one of Chad Preston's columns, but rather a news story under Preston's byline that we are running on page one with a two-column headline that reads 'Dunagan Blasts Print Attack on Cramer!' Here is the article, word for word:

> *Grocery magnate and recently appointed Police Review*
> *Board member Weldon Dunagan today decried a report in*

another New York newspaper that Inspector Lionel T. Cra-
mer of the Homicide Squad had been seen dining privately
with mob boss Ralph Mars in a Little Italy restaurant.

"I find this piece of so-called journalism to be spuri-
ous and irresponsible, as well as an unfounded attack
upon one of the department's longest-serving and most-
decorated officers," Mr. Dunagan said. "I have directed the
Police Review Board to initiate an investigation into the
source of this scurrilous item."

Police Commissioner Daniel J. O'Hara joined Mr.
Dunagan in denouncing the news item, saying, "This is an
insult to Mr. Cramer, who has every right to sue."

For his part, Inspector Cramer said, "My record speaks
for itself." Mr. Mars did not respond to numerous attempts
to reach him for a comment.

"Okay, there it is," Lon said.

"Mr. Cohen, I note the inspector did not deny that a meeting with Ralph Mars took place," Wolfe said.

"I thought you would pick up on that."

"It seems to me you have stacked the deck, to use one of Archie's favorite terms, against Mr. Rowcliff."

"Do you deny that he has it coming?" Lon asked.

"I do not," Wolfe said. "I assume disciplinary action will be brought against the captain."

"Almost surely, and it well may be the end of his career. He hitched his wagon to the wrong star, specifically the *Journal-American* and its second-rate columnist, if I may be allowed to crow."

"I for one would not deny you that pleasure, Mr. Cohen. I hope you will avail yourself of the opportunity to join us for dinner in the very near future. Archie will be issuing an invitation."

"That is an invitation I look forward to receiving," Lon said.

"Well, what's next?" I asked Wolfe after we had hung up.

"Call Mr. Cramer. Before all this foofaraw over dueling newspaper articles erupted, the inspector proposed a meeting, saying he had an inkling as to the identity of Mr. Pierce's murderer. Let us learn whether his inkling matches my own."

"So you've got an inkling of your own?"

"I do, and have had for some time. But I am not about to argue over whether we each have the same idea, and if we do, who came up with it first."

I picked up the phone to call Cramer, but before I could begin dialing, the doorbell rang. "Hah! No need for the telephone, we both know who that is," I told Wolfe as I left the office and headed down the hall to the front door.

"Good afternoon," I said to Cramer, who stepped inside without a word and walked slowly down the hall to the office. He sat in the red leather chair and nodded to his host.

"We were about to call you, sir," Wolfe said. "Mr. Cohen read us the article about you that will be running in this afternoon's later editions of the *Gazette*."

"Yeah, he read it to me as well," Cramer said in a subdued tone. "Nice of him. But, of course, I'm sure he knows the truth about me and Mars having that dinner, just as you do."

"You have no reason to be chagrined," Wolfe said. "Your motives and intentions were good. As Archie likes to say about basketball, 'no harm, no foul.'"

"Thanks for that," the inspector said, sounding like he meant it. "What I can't figure out is how two people—O'Hara and Dunagan—who were out to get me now defend me, and in print, no less. They suddenly are in my corner. It makes no sense, not that I'm complaining."

"People sometimes have epiphanies, as it is written that Paul did on the Damascus Road. There is often no explaining the human animal," Wolfe said.

"I suppose so," Cramer replied. "I have no idea what will to happen to Rowcliff, and at the moment, I'm not sure that I even care. I defended the man for years, even when he made an ass of himself, which was more than once. But dammit, he was as brave as a bear. He could have been a great cop."

"Perhaps, but I believe you would be better off not dwelling on what might have been. Some people are their own worst enemy, and this would seem to be the case with Mr. Rowcliff."

"I guess you're right," the inspector replied, shaking his head. For whatever reasons, he had not once pulled out a cigar to gnaw on.

"You told Archie you have an inkling, that is the word you used, as to who murdered Lester Pierce," Wolfe said. "I am interested in your choice."

Cramer reached into his breast pocket and pulled out a sheet of paper and a pen and scribbled something, handing the sheet to Wolfe, who read it and gave his thin-lipped version of a smile. "We are of one mind, sir," he said. I went around behind him and looked over his shoulder at the name the inspector had printed. Maybe by now you have guessed the identity, but I had not, although the individual was one of three possibilities on my own list.

"We are in agreement," Cramer said. "I have a proposal."

Wolfe dipped his chin and said nothing. The inspector had the floor.

"You have been damned effective over the years with what I like to call your charades. Now it is my turn to host one."

I think that took my boss by surprise, although he remained silent, leaning back in his chair, hands interlaced over his middle mound. I am not sure if he knew what was coming next, but I know I didn't.

"All right," Cramer continued, leaning forward, resting his arms on his knees, and focusing directly on Wolfe. "There is a pleasant enough conference room at Centre Street, although nothing like this," he said, looking around the office. "But it will do for my purposes."

"What are your purposes?" Wolfe asked.

"To gather all the suspects together—along with whomever else you choose—while we, you and I, name the murderer."

I could not believe my ears. Cramer was actually suggesting that Wolfe leave home in the brownstone and venture forth to police headquarters on Centre Street blocks away in Lower Manhattan.

"When do you propose such a meeting would take place?"

"As soon as I am able to round up all the key people in this case—Dunagan, Marchbank, Miss Cordwell, Pierce's widow, and her three children."

"How do you go about persuading each of these people to appear in a group?"

"I suppose the same way you persuade them to come here in a group to unveil a killer. I can also be persuasive," Cramer said contentiously.

Wolfe leaned back and considered the inspector from barely open eyes. "Sir, if you are able to bring these individuals together in your offices, I will be present for the denouement you are planning."

For the second time in the space of a minute or so, I was stunned, although I tried not to show it. I looked at Wolfe, who pointedly ignored me.

"Then it's a deal," Cramer said. "Would you like to make any additions to the guest list?"

"No, it appears complete. Now as to logistics: Will you have a chair that accommodates me?"

"You can count on it," Cramer said, rubbing his palms together.

Wearing a self-satisfied grin, the inspector walked out with a spring in his gait. After locking the front door behind him, I returned to the office. "What game are you playing?" I demanded to Wolfe.

"Game? I am not participating in any game," he replied, looking up at me with eyes now wide open.

"Oh, now I get it," I said, sliding into my desk chair and slapping my forehead with a palm. "You know damned well that Cramer won't be able to get every one of them in the same room at the same time."

"I know nothing of the kind, Archie. In fact, were I a betting man like you, I would gamble a sizable percentage of my holdings that Mr. Cramer will be successful in prevailing upon each of the seven to attend his assemblage."

"Hell, you could just as easily have worked things to have the whole business held right here like you usually do."

"Perhaps, but Mr. Cramer and I reached the same conclusion, and it is possible he arrived at it before I did. In any event, he has earned the right to oversee the proceedings. I will not begrudge him that opportunity."

"I just can't believe I am hearing this. You do not have to save Cramer's bacon, if that's your intent. He has already been exonerated, if that's the right word, by both Commissioner O'Hara and Weldon Dunagan, he of the Police Review Board. Do you mean to tell me you are really going all the way down to 240 Centre Street, that tired old police headquarters that ought to be replaced, where you will have no beer and will be forced to sit in a chair you will detest, despite what Cramer says, all the while listening to him pontificate?"

"The inspector may pontificate," Wolfe conceded, "but I assure you I will do my share of the talking as well. And by the way, although I haven't said it, you also will be present."

"Yeah, somehow I already had figured as much. You are going to need a chauffeur to take you all the way down to the wilds of deepest Lower Manhattan, and it might as well be me, right?"

"You have framed the program most succinctly," Wolfe said, pulling the platinum pocket watch out of his vest pocket and glancing at it. "It is three minutes past the time for me to board the elevator."

CHAPTER 28

For more than two days, we heard nothing from Inspector Cramer, and I found myself chuckling inwardly. As I had suspected would happen, he probably was unable to pull together a gathering of those most closely involved in the Pierce murder case.

Then came a call on a rainy Thursday morning. "Goodwin, we are set for tomorrow night," Cramer snapped. "Nine o'clock in Room 317 at Centre Street. I made it that time because I know Wolfe's schedule, and that hour won't interfere with either a meal or one of those twice-a-day visits with his precious orchids."

"And everybody said they'd be there?"

"Yep. It took a little persuading, particularly with Marchbank and both of the Pierce sons, but I wore them down. I figured Dunagan would be a tough sell, but the man surprised me and said to count him in. He wanted to know exactly what was going to happen, and I told him he would have to wait and see."

"I'm sure he wasn't wild about that."

"No, but he badly wants to see this business cleared up for the good of the department. Like the rest of us, he is sick and tired of all the newspaper attacks on the police."

"Do you have a chair that will suit Mr. Wolfe? You know how he can be."

Cramer snorted. "I am bringing a chair from O'Hara's office, which is almost as big as the one in your boss's office in the brownstone."

"Speaking of the commissioner, did he ask to be present tomorrow?"

"It did not come up," Cramer said. "He is on vacation again, somewhere down south in the warmth. He doesn't even know about this meeting, and I'm not about to tell him. If he comes back angry that he missed all the fun, Dunagan can calm him down. After all, the commissioner does report to the Police Board."

"Good point. When Wolfe descends from communing with the orchids, I will fill him in, although don't be surprised if he's changed his mind and has decided to skip your party."

"He had better not be absent," Cramer said sharply. "It is important that he and I present a united front."

"I will be sure to tell him," I said. When Wolfe did come down from on high, I gave him the details. "Cramer says he's got a chair that will suit you. It's from Commissioner O'Hara's office."

He grunted and rang for beer, then riffled through the day's mail, which I had stacked on his desk blotter.

"Are you really going through with this?" I asked.

The answer I got was a glare, after which Wolfe uncapped the first of two beers Fritz had just brought in on a tray along with the usual chilled pilsner glass.

"You haven't inquired as to whether I am available to chauffeur you down to Centre Street tomorrow night."

"Well?" he demanded, glaring again.

"All right, since you have asked, yes, I am available. I had contemplated inviting Lily Rowan to dinner at Rusterman's, but on reflection, I could not imagine you having to ride thirty-plus blocks in a New York taxi. That is simply too frightening to contemplate."

After yet a third glare, Wolfe finished the mail and picked up his latest book, *Only in America* by Harry Golden, while I began typing the correspondence Wolfe had dictated the day before. I had finished only one letter when the telephone rang. It was Lon Cohen.

"I worry when I don't hear from you for several days," he said. "Is there something that I should know?"

"I believe it is fair to say some news may be forthcoming regarding the Lester Pierce killing."

"When?"

"Soon, maybe within the next day or so, but don't hold me to that."

"Archie, we've been working with you on this. The *Gazette* has earned the right to a scoop, and you know it."

"Patience, my friend, and you will very possibly be rewarded."

"What's this 'very possibly' claptrap, private snoop? Have the two of you switched your allegiance to another newspaper?"

"How can you say that after what we've been through together over the years? Remember all the good times?"

"But what have you done for me lately?" Lon asked.

"Some people are never happy." I sighed. "Well, you will just have to trust in us and hope for the best."

"Why is it that I am not encouraged by your words?"

"Stay tuned," I said. "Now I must say good-bye. I believe it is fair to say you will be hearing from us again, possibly in the next two days. Will you be in your office late tomorrow night?"

"I am always in the office late, as you damned well know," he said.

"That's good to hear. Stay close to your phone."

Lon started to reply, but his words were cut off when I cradled my phone.

CHAPTER 29

Anyone who chanced to be walking or driving along a certain block of West Thirty-Fifth Street at a quarter past eight that Friday night would have been treated to the sight of Nero Wolfe, clad in a gray overcoat with fur collar, wearing a black felt hat and carrying his red-thorn walking stick, coming deliberately down the steps of the brownstone and climbing into the backseat of a Heron sedan idling in front.

I was at the wheel of the Heron. As I pulled smoothly away from the curb, I looked in the rearview mirror and saw Wolfe tightly grasp the leather strap that had been retrofitted onto the car on his orders. On the rare occasions when he ventures forth from the brownstone—to the barber, the Metropolitan Orchid Show, or out to Louis Hewitt's Long Island mansion once a year for dinner—Wolfe will ride in a vehicle driven only by me or, on rare occasions, by Saul Panzer. Even then, he rarely speaks, clenches his teeth, and never relaxes.

When I am driving Wolfe, I make a point of not talking because he feels I am incapable of piloting the car and jawing at the same time. I drove downtown at a far slower speed than when I am alone, and I never ran an amber light. We pulled up at the front door of the old, domed building at 240 Centre Street whose architecture was better suited to a European city than to New York.

I parked, daring a ticket, and opened the back door for Wolfe, who climbed out and walked the few steps to the arched doorway, his stick tapping a beat on the pavement. We went through the marble lobby with its coffered ceiling and took an unoccupied elevator to the third floor. Room 317 obviously was used for conferences. It was spartan, hardly unusual in a police building, with a long table that had four chairs on each side and one at each end. As it was only 8:35, the room was empty except for one person: Sergeant Purley Stebbins.

"Mr. Wolfe," he said stiffly, "the inspector suggested you sit here." He gestured to a well-padded chair with arms that was placed off to one side of the seat at what appeared to be the head of the table. "The inspector will be next to you." The sergeant turned to me. "And you can sit behind Mr. Wolfe," he added, managing to avoid calling me by name.

Wolfe settled into his designated chair, finding it to be adequate, although less than comfortable. "I need to say something," Purley told him. "While we are here alone, I want to thank you for all you have done for the inspector."

"You are too generous with your gratitude," Wolfe remarked. "Mr. Cramer has once again shown he is able to protect himself adequately. He did not need assistance from me."

Purley's expression indicated he did not believe the denial, but he made no response. At that moment, the door swung open and Roland Marchbank stepped in, peering around grimly as though he had wandered into the wrong place—until he spotted me.

"You! What are you doing here? I thought this was a police meeting." Then he noticed Wolfe. "Just what in the hell is going on?" he asked Stebbins, who was wearing his usual rumpled brown suit. "Are you an officer?"

"I am a sergeant, sir," Purley said. "The inspector will explain everything when he comes in. Please take a seat anywhere you wish."

As Marchbank slid into a chair, the door opened again, and Audra and Marianne Pierce entered the room, looking first at me and then at Wolfe. Audra nodded at Wolfe, then whispered in her daughter's ear, probably telling her the identity of the very large man in the yellow shirt and brown, vested suit.

Purley played host once again, telling the women to sit wherever they chose, as Audra turned and gave a reserved nod and a whispered hello to Marchbank, to whom she introduced Marianne. He stood and shook her hand, favoring the young woman with a tight-lipped smile, the only kind he apparently possessed.

The next two members of the Pierce family also arrived in tandem, brothers Malcolm and Mark, each wearing a suit and tie and providing a study in contrasts. Malcolm sauntered in self-assured and with a grin, while his younger sibling wore a frown that competed with Marchbank's own dour countenance.

As they were getting themselves seated, the former Miss Missouri made her entry, looking even more self-possessed than Malcolm Pierce. All that practice prancing on beauty pageant runways in high heels undoubtedly contributed to Laura Cordwell's grace and poise. Her smile definitely contained an element of irony as she chose a seat at the table directly across from the widow Pierce, who eyed her unblinking and with a cool detachment.

The last of the guests, Weldon Dunagan, came in seconds after Laura. He looked first at Wolfe, then scanned the seated assemblage and chose a chair between Laura and Roland Marchbank.

"Where's Cramer?" Dunagan barked. "It looks to me like everybody else is here."

"They are, Mr. Dunagan," the inspector said. He had come in through a side door and strode to his place at the head of the table. He wore a navy blue double-breasted suit that fit him perfectly. I had never seen the man so well garbed.

As I took in the scene, I realized we were in some sort of parallel universe, a complete reversal of one of Wolfe's assemblages in the brownstone. Cramer was playing the role of Wolfe, and Purley Stebbins was cast as me, while Wolfe had become Cramer and I was—you guessed it—Stebbins.

"Thank you all for coming tonight," the inspector said as he sat. "Now I—"

"Now just hold on a minute!" Marchbank interrupted. "I want to know what those two are doing here?" he demanded, pointing at Wolfe and me.

"They are Nero Wolfe and Archie Goodwin, and—"

"We know very well who they are," Marchbank said. "What I want to know is *why* they are here."

Cramer glowered at him. "If I may be allowed to complete a sentence, sir, they are present at my request and have been most helpful in this investigation."

"This is damned unorthodox," Marchbank persisted as he shifted in his chair.

"Then by all means mark me as unorthodox; I have been called far worse over the years. Does anyone here have objections to their being present?" Cramer looked from face to face around the table and got no response.

"Very well, we will continue. I have identified Messrs. Wolfe and Goodwin. Around the table, starting clockwise on my left, are Malcolm Pierce; his brother, Mark; their mother, Audra; and her daughter, Marianne. On the other side, after the empty chair, are Laura Cordwell of the Good Government Group, Weldon Dunagan of DunaganMarts, who is also a member of the Police Review Board, and on my immediate right, Roland Marchbank, also of the Good Government Group. Are there any questions?"

"I have one," Mark Pierce said heatedly. "How was the so-called guest list put together?"

"A legitimate question," Cramer answered. "Each of you had a close relationship with Lester Pierce, and one or more of you may be able to shed some light on the cause of his death."

Cramer's statement set off a flurry of heated conversation, with everyone talking at once, either to one another or to the inspector. As the pandemonium finally died down, Malcolm Pierce spoke: "Pardon my puzzlement, but from the beginning it has seemed obvious to me that the crime syndicate was behind my father's death, as I have so stated on several occasions. I still hold to that belief. What reason do any of you have to think otherwise?"

"As has been stated by numerous individuals—myself included—what did the syndicate really have to fear from the Good Government Group? Three-G had been hammering away at the mob for years with little or no success," Cramer replied.

"Now it is true that the man who in all probability shot Lester Pierce was a mob triggerman named Guido Capelli," the inspector continued. "But Capelli himself was shot dead mob-style a few days later, and by the very people he supposedly worked for. The apparent reason: he had a reputation for taking on outside jobs, jobs definitely not sanctioned by his bosses.

"They did not like that because, one, he was making money on the side, and two, the syndicate was getting blamed for murders they did not commit. We learned that Capelli had been warned before, but he kept on going rogue. The killing of Mr. Pierce was the last straw."

"I definitely do not subscribe to the mob being behind Lester's death," Marchbank said, "but do they really care whether they get blamed for killings that they have nothing to do with?"

"A good point, but oddly enough, some of these mobsters have a rather skewed ethical standard," Cramer responded. "They feel that their own hits are justified, but they don't approve of other people hiring killers."

"Okay, so if we are to assume that the syndicate did not target my father, just who did?" Marianne Pierce asked.

Cramer turned to Wolfe, nodding. "Each of you in this room was interviewed by one or more of us—Mr. Cramer, Mr. Goodwin, and me," Wolfe said, adjusting his bulk in the almost adequate chair.

"Yeah, and I was lucky enough to sit down with all three of you at one time or another," Marchbank put in testily.

"Correct," Wolfe responded. "Each of those around this table with one notable exception has conceded that the crime syndicate was not behind the shooting of Mr. Pierce." With that, they all looked to their left, their right, and across the table. The room became deadly quiet.

Weldon Dunagan tugged at his silk necktie and cleared his throat. "All right, I think you and the inspector have strung this out long enough," he said. "Are you going to accuse someone or not?"

"First, I would like to learn whether anyone has something they would like to say before I continue," Wolfe responded. "We are in no hurry."

"I disagree," Mark Pierce said. "I believe I speak for everyone here when I claim we all, every one of us, would like to leave as soon as possible. Nothing has been accomplished here tonight."

"Does everyone agree with Mr. Mark Pierce?" Wolfe asked. "How about the other Mr. Pierce?"

Malcolm swallowed hard, his earlier bonhomie gone. "What do you want me to say?" he asked in a hoarse voice.

"Whatever you like," Wolfe said.

Malcolm jumped up. "Damn all of you!" he said in a suddenly high-pitched tone. "Particularly my brother and sister. You both stood by while my mother here had to put up with her husband's philandering—and with you among others," he rasped, pointing a shaky index finger at Laura Cordwell, who recoiled as if having been slapped.

Audra Pierce audibly drew in air and tensed as her daughter put an arm around her. "I do not believe what you are trying to say," she told her son. "I don't believe a word of it."

"Believe it, Mother!" Malcolm yelled, still on his feet, hyperventilating and with the veins standing out in his neck.

"Mr. Goodwin paid a visit to Marcantonio, the brother of Guido Capelli, who shot Lester Pierce," Wolfe cut in. "He stated Guido was hired by 'somebody rich who lived good.'"

"Every one of us in this room is what you might term rich," Audra said calmly.

"As far as riches go, I am hardly in the same league with the rest of you!" Marchbank barked.

"Now, really, Roland, you would be considered wealthy by most standards," Audra countered.

"Let us stipulate that all of you are 'financially comfortable,' however one chooses to define that term," Wolfe said, "although some among you live in particularly lavish surroundings." He turned toward Malcolm Pierce. "Perhaps Mr. Capelli had occasion to visit you at your residence in the Dakota, which Mr. Goodwin informs me is luxurious."

"No, I would never have invited him up to—" Malcolm froze in midsentence, but it was too late, and he knew it. For several seconds, the room was dead silent, broken by shocked gasps from Lester Pierce's mother and daughter, the color having drained from their faces.

Audra stared at her eldest son, shaking her head as if in disbelief. Her usual controlled demeanor had begun to crumble.

"All right, now you all know!" Malcolm keened, rocking on the balls of his feet and looking at the ceiling. "I did it for you, Mother, for you. I couldn't stand what he was doing to you. I would do it again, by God, yes I would! It was the only thing I could do. Do you hear me?"

I suddenly realized I had just witnessed the first rehearsal of a defendant who was aiming for an insanity plea. Malcolm's acting needed work, although a jury might just buy his performance.

Cramer gestured to Purley Stebbins, who went behind Malcolm and began to read him the new Miranda rights as he helped him to his feet and led him out of the room without resistance.

The rest of the group appeared to be in some sort of communal trance until Weldon Dunagan spoke. "Bear in mind that what just happened here tonight does not in any way make this a court of law, nor should it be thought of as such. We live in a society where one is considered innocent until proven guilty."

High-minded words, but they did little to console any of the three Pierces, who stood huddled together in silence. As for Roland Marchbank, he continued to wear a frown. Whether it was from anger or frustration was difficult to discern. And it was clear Laura Cordwell could feel the general animosity toward her, and she walked out of the room as quietly as possible. Cramer and Dunagan stood in one corner talking in hushed tones, probably hashing over the events of the evening.

I turned to Wolfe, who had gotten to his feet and wore a scowl. "It is time for us to go home," I said, and he did not disagree.

Not a word was spoken on the drive north. I dropped Wolfe off at the front steps of the brownstone and drove the car to Curran's, pulling it into the big garage. When I returned home, he had gone up to bed.

I settled in at my desk and dialed a number I knew by heart. "Yeah?" Lon Cohen snapped.

"My advice to you is to call Cramer immediately. He will still be in his office. I believe you will find the effort worthwhile."

"Whoa! What can you tell me first?"

"I can tell you that Wolfe and I spent the evening at Centre Street tonight, along with a number of other people."

"Wolfe, all the way down at Centre Street? Are you putting me on?"

"I am not. Call Cramer." I hung up before he could pepper me with questions.

CHAPTER 30

The next morning as I walked into the kitchen for breakfast, a frown creased Fritz's face. "What is troubling you, oh master chef?" I asked as he handed me a plate of scrambled eggs, Canadian bacon, and a blueberry muffin.

"Mr. Wolfe is in a bad mood this morning, Archie. He received a telephone call from Mr. Cohen and had to speak with him for several minutes."

"I must have been in the shower at the time. I know he does not like his morning routine upset, and I hope the call did not affect his appetite."

"When I went up a few minutes ago, his plates and dishes were clean."

"Thank heavens. That being the case, the time he spent on the telephone could not have been too traumatic."

I went into the office with coffee and dialed Lon at the

Gazette. "I understand you talked to my boss this morning," I told him.

"Yeah, and at first he didn't seem overly happy to hear from me."

"You disturbed his routine, which always makes him grumpy. I'm just surprised he didn't bite your head off."

"He actually was very helpful once he got over the irritation of being interrupted at breakfast," Lon said. "I got some good quotes from him about what happened last night, and they will help with the dandy page story in our early edition that you'll get delivered on your doorstep before noon. A story, I hasten to add, that will be an exclusive. We don't run into alleged patricide cases every day."

"I'm happy for you. What did my boss have to say?"

"One thing really surprised me, Archie. He seemed eager to give the lion's share of the credit for nailing Malcolm Pierce to Inspector Cramer."

"Really?"

"Yes, really. Here is one of his quotes: 'I am pleased I could be of some assistance to Inspector Cramer in this endeavor.'"

"A newfound modesty," I observed.

"Whatever you want to call it, Cramer really comes out as a winner. I also talked to Weldon Dunagan in his capacity as a member of the Police Review Board, and he too praised the inspector. 'It is a benefit to the entire city to have Mr. Cramer back as head of the Homicide Squad,' he said. That must have been some scene down on Centre Street last night."

"It was. Cramer in a brand-new suit that must have set him back some real dollars, Wolfe squeezing into a chair at least one size too small for him, and Stebbins waiting to pounce on someone, anyone. I wish I'd had a camera."

"Me too," Lon said. "It will be interesting to see how the courts handle Malcolm Pierce. Do you think his lawyers will go for an insanity plea?"

"I suppose that's possible, even likely. I had only met him once before, and he seemed like the picture of sanity to me. But last night was another story. He started coming unhinged, although that might have been by design."

"Adding to the drama is that he lives in the Dakota. We're running a photo of that historic old castle along with a mug shot of Malcolm," Lon said.

"You sound as enthusiastic as the kid who just pulled his favorite toy out of a Cracker Jack box."

"Getting scoops never grows old for me, Archie. Every time I think about retiring, a story like this one comes along, and it makes me remember why I got into this crazy business in the first place."

"Glad we could help rekindle your youth," I told him. "Just don't do anything rash, like buying yourself a pair of roller skates."

"Thanks for reminding me to act my age. Now I've got to go to the newsroom and see how they're coming with the layout of page one."

I wished Lon well and turned to the orchid germination records our plant nurse, Theodore Horstmann, had brought down from upstairs. They had to be entered on file cards, one of my least-favorite tasks. I had almost finished when the phone rang, and I answered.

"This is Audra Pierce, Mr. Goodwin. I would like to make an appointment to see Mr. Wolfe today," she said in a quiet but firm voice.

"He is not available at the moment, but I can have him get back to you later this morning."

"That would be fine," she replied. "I await his call."

. . .

When Wolfe came down from the plant rooms at eleven, rang for beer, and got himself settled, I swiveled to face him. "Quite a night, wasn't it?"

He frowned at me but said nothing, so I pushed on. "Mrs. Pierce telephoned earlier and wants to see you."

His face reflected surprise. "What does she want?"

"She did not say. Do you want me to call the lady and find out what's on her mind?"

"No," he said with a sigh. "Have her come at three."

I reached her and gave her the time, which she said was agreeable. "This hardly figures to be a joyful meeting, does it?" I asked Wolfe.

He again said nothing and turned to the stack of mail from the morning delivery that I had placed on his desk blotter. No more words were spoken between us until lunch, which happened to be fine by me.

We were back in the office when the doorbell rang two minutes before three. Even with her drawn expression, Audra Kingston Pierce looked regal. I could not begin to imagine how she must be feeling.

"Please come in," I said, holding the door for her.

"Good afternoon, Mr. Goodwin," she said with a nod as I hung her mink on the hall rack and followed her down the corridor to the office.

"Mr. Wolfe," she said as she slipped into the red leather chair. "Thank you for seeing me."

I could tell that my boss was at a loss for words, so he simply nodded.

"Well, you were correct with what you said when first we

met," she told him. "When I hired you, you warned me that—and I think I have the quote right—'My findings might not satisfy you, for a variety of reasons.' Do you recall saying those words?"

"I do."

"Well, you certainly were right. The decision that you and Inspector Cramer came up with was by no means a satisfying one, but I do not quarrel with it. I now want to pay you the rest of our agreed-upon amount." She pulled a checkbook and pen from her purse.

"If you please, madam," Wolfe said, "Inspector Cramer and I independently arrived at the same conclusion, as you just suggested, so I am hardly entitled to the balance of the commission."

"Well, I can hardly give it to the inspector, can I? That probably would violate all sorts of laws. No, you have definitely earned this," she said, writing out a check and placing it on his desk. "I must insist."

Wolfe nodded again, a tacit acceptance of the money. "What are your plans now?" he asked.

"My son is still my son, and I am going to obtain the best lawyer possible for him. I already have been in touch with two attorneys, and I am not done looking, I assure you. Also, I want you to know that I bear you no ill will whatever because of what has occurred. We must live with the world as it is, not as we would wish it to be."

"Well spoken, madam. I agree completely."

"I doubt very much we will have occasion to ever meet again, but despite the pain all of this has caused me, I appreciate what you have done." She stood and held out a hand to Wolfe, which to my surprise he took. To my greater surprise, he actually rose as she turned to leave!

I walked Audra down the hall to the front door, and as she

left, I said, "Nero Wolfe rarely shakes hands, particularly with a woman, and he almost never stands in one's presence."

"Well, then there is hope for him yet, isn't there?" she said as I detected a slight twinkle in her eye.

Back in the office, I sat and said to Wolfe, "Correct me if I am wrong, but I believe neither you nor Inspector Cramer was absolutely convinced of Malcolm Pierce's guilt until you tricked him with that comment of yours about the Dakota."

Wolfe looked at me evenly but said nothing.

CHAPTER 31

As of this writing, Malcolm Pierce's trial remains in the courts, where there have been numerous continuances and countless objections on both sides. His lawyers have argued that Pierce cannot be charged with murder because there is no evidence that he ever hired Guido Capelli, despite his confession-like behavior that night at Centre Street.

As persuasive as his lawyers are—and his mother got him some very good ones—the current district attorney is no slouch either, and his own performance in court is probably driven at least in part by the fact that he has political ambitions. Lon Cohen feels the trial could go on for years.

Roland Marchbank ended up getting the top spot at the Good Government Group, in large measure because of the support from Weldon Dunagan. Marchbank has hired an assistant, a young man only a few years out of Harvard who has been dubbed the "Cambridge Whiz" by members of the press.

Laura Cordwell, who saw her chance to run Three-G go up in smoke, switched careers and now is employed by one of the local television stations as a weekend anchor. She started out as a reporter for the station and quickly got promoted. The TV critic for the *Gazette* has written that "it is only a matter of time before the fetching Miss Cordwell will be anointed as one of the eleven o'clock anchors for the channel, and remember, you read it here first."

Hers seems an unusual choice for a brilliant young woman with a business degree and high honors from an Ivy League university, but television has a reputation for paying its most visible personalities extremely well. And if the gossip columnists know what they are talking about, it appears she has found herself a regular escort in the form of a New York Yankees outfielder who has been dubbed "Manhattan's Most Eligible Bachelor" by a local magazine. "Could This Be Our Town's New Power Couple?" a headline in one of the tabloids posed.

Mark Pierce has himself been in the news of late. He recently won an award from one of the advertising publications for the campaign he was working on for that brand of coffee when I visited him at his home in Dobbs Ferry. A picture in the *Times* showed him holding up his statuette at the awards presentation beside his attractive wife, who looked on with an adoring smile.

I ran into Mark's sister, Marianne, recently at a black-tie banquet honoring women that I attended with Lily Rowan at the Waldorf. Lily received a plaque for her work with a local orphanage, while Marianne also was honored for having persuaded her fashion magazine to sponsor a girls' club for underprivileged teens. The two women got along just like old friends at the cocktail reception before the dinner.

When Marianne went off to join the others from her magazine at their table for dinner, Lily turned to me. "A very attractive and intelligent young woman, wouldn't you say, Escamillo?"

"Yes, she is quite nice-looking."

"*Nice-looking?* She's a knockout, and you know it. Or am I missing something between you here?"

"Not at all. I got to know her because it was part of the job, that's all."

"For some strange reason, I believe you," Lily said. "It's time for the dinner to begin."

Weldon Dunagan continued to make news in the grocery business. DunaganMarts bought up its largest competitor, and the business magazines proclaimed him the biggest thing that had happened in the food industry since sliced bread came on the market in 1928.

This narrative would not be complete without mention of Police Commissioner Daniel J. O'Hara. He returned home from his latest warm-weather vacation to learn that the Pierce murder case was headed for the courtroom. He had little choice but to praise Inspector Cramer for his work on the investigation.

For his part, the inspector was suitably modest, thanking Nero Wolfe for the role he had played. "We have often worked together," Cramer said to a *Gazette* reporter. Wolfe was unavailable for comment.

CHAPTER 32

This morning, as I sat in the office after breakfast typing Wolfe's correspondence from the day before, Fritz walked in wearing a puzzled expression. "The man from Fallon's Liquors just dropped off two cases of Mr. Wolfe's beer," he said.

"So what's the problem?" I asked. "That happens every few days."

"But, Archie, this was not on our schedule. We just got a shipment yesterday. We aren't to get another one until next week. I asked Stan, the deliveryman, about it and he just shrugged. I don't want us to get overbilled," Fritz said. He is always protective of our finances.

"I'll call Fallon's," I told him, picking up the phone. "Hi, Eddie, Archie Goodwin here. Stan just delivered two cases of Remmers that we hadn't ordered. Are you trying to get Mr. Wolfe to increase his capacity? It's already off the charts."

"No, Archie, this was extra. It was paid for by someone who wants to be anonymous."

"Really? Care to tell me who it is?"

"Sorry, you know I can't do that."

"Does the last name begin with 'C'?"

I heard a slight cough on the other end, confirming my suspicion, and I decided against questioning Eddie further. He's got his scruples, and I don't want to mess with them. I also decided not to say anything to Wolfe about the bonus delivery. Leave it to him to figure out the identity of his benefactor. After all, he is a genius.

AUTHOR NOTES

This story is set in the second decade after the midpoint of the twentieth century, and most of its settings, with the notable exception of Nero Wolfe's brownstone on West Thirty-Fifth Street, are accurately placed within the New York area.

The Dakota Apartments, on Manhattan's Upper West Side, where Archie Goodwin meets Malcolm Pierce, is a historic landmark that was completed in 1884. With its peaked roofs, gables, dormers, balconies, and balustrades, the structure has been architecturally termed North German Renaissance.

The Dakota has been home to many noted personalities, among them Lauren Bacall, Judy Garland, Leonard Bernstein, Rudolf Nureyev, Boris Karloff, Jason Robards, Connie Chung, Rosemary Clooney, Gilda Radner, and football's Joe Namath. Another resident, the Beatles' John Lennon, was shot dead outside the building in 1980.

The Dakota also has been the site of several motion pictures, including *Vanilla Sky* with Tom Cruise and *Rosemary's Baby* with Mia Farrow. The 1970 illustrated novel *Time and Again* by Jack Finney also was set at the Dakota.

240 Centre Street, in Lower Manhattan, where the climax of this story takes place, served as New York City's police headquarters from 1909 to 1973, when it was replaced by a fourteen-story building done in the brutalist architectural style and named One Police Plaza, also in Lower Manhattan. The baroque 240 Centre Street structure was converted to luxury residences in 1988.

The Greenpoint Hospital in Brooklyn, where Saul Panzer recuperates from his beating, opened in 1914 and continued to be used until 1982, when it was replaced by Woodhull Hospital, also in Brooklyn. Some of the Greenpoint campus buildings have been converted to affordable housing units.

All the newspapers referred to existed in the New York of the day with the exception of the *Gazette*, which has played a role in many of the Nero Wolfe stories over the years, along with its longtime employee Lon Cohen. He has been a regular in these tales and one of the paper's editors, although neither Mr. Stout nor I have ever given him a specific title at the *Gazette*. Cohen clearly has a lot of influence at the paper, however. The *Journal-American*, whose fictional columnist in our story attempts to smear Inspector Cramer, was a Hearst-owned afternoon newspaper that in 1966 merged with two other New York dailies, the *World Telegram and Sun* and the *Herald Tribune* to form the *World Journal Tribune*. The merged newspaper folded in 1967.

The Good Government Group mentioned throughout the book is fictional, although similar nonprofit organizations working against organized crime and civic corruption have existed in numerous large American cities. One example is Chicago's long-running Better Government Association.

Similar to my previous books, I have relied on several sources, particularly these three: *Nero Wolfe of West Thirty-Fifth Street: The Life and Times of America's Largest Private Detective* by William Baring-Gould (The Viking Press, New York, 1968); *The Nero Wolfe Cookbook* by Rex Stout and the Editors of Viking Press (Viking Press, New York, 1973); and *Rex Stout: A Biography* by John McAleer (Little, Brown & Co., Boston, 1977). The McAleer volume justly won an Edgar Award in the biography category from the Mystery Writers of America.

As with my past books, I send my sincere regards to Barbara Stout and Rebecca Bradbury Stout, the daughters of the late Rex Stout. They have been consistently encouraging of my efforts to reimagine the wonderful stories, characters, and milieus created by their father and continued by him for four decades.

My thanks and appreciation goes to my agent, Martha Kaplan, to Otto Penzler and Rob Hart of Mysterious Press, and to the fine team at Open Road Integrated Media.

And my warmest thanks of all go to my wife, Janet, who has provided me with unconditional love and support for more than a half century.

ABOUT THE AUTHOR

Robert Goldsborough is an American author best known for continuing Rex Stout's famous Nero Wolfe series. Born in Chicago, he attended Northwestern University and upon graduation went to work for the Associated Press, beginning a lifelong career in journalism that would include long periods at the *Chicago Tribune* and *Advertising Age*.

While at the *Tribune*, Goldsborough began writing mysteries in the voice of Rex Stout, the creator of iconic sleuths Nero Wolfe and Archie Goodwin. Goldsborough's first novel starring Wolfe, *Murder in E Minor* (1986), was met with acclaim from both critics and devoted fans, winning a Nero Award from the Wolfe Pack. Eleven more Wolfe mysteries followed, including

Death on Deadline (1987) and *Fade to Black* (1990). In 2005, Goldsborough published *Three Strikes You're Dead*, the first in an original series starring Chicago Tribune reporter Snap Malek. *The Battered Badge* (2018) is his most recent novel.

THE NERO WOLFE MYSTERIES

FROM MYSTERIOUSPRESS.COM
AND OPEN ROAD MEDIA

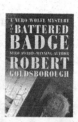

MYSTERIOUSPRESS.COM

Otto Penzler, owner of the Mysterious Bookshop in Manhattan, founded the Mysterious Press in 1975. Penzler quickly became known for his outstanding selection of mystery, crime, and suspense books, both from his imprint and in his store. The imprint was devoted to printing the best books in these genres, using fine paper and top dust-jacket artists, as well as offering many limited, signed editions.

Now the Mysterious Press has gone digital, publishing ebooks through **MysteriousPress.com**.

MysteriousPress.com offers readers essential noir and suspense fiction, hard-boiled crime novels, and the latest thrillers from both debut authors and mystery masters. Discover classics and new voices, all from one legendary source.

FIND OUT MORE AT

WWW.MYSTERIOUSPRESS.COM

FOLLOW US:

@emysteries and Facebook.com/MysteriousPressCom

MysteriousPress.com is one of a select group of publishing partners of Open Road Integrated Media, Inc.

THE MYSTERIOUS BOOKSHOP, founded in 1979, is located in Manhattan's Tribeca neighborhood. It is the oldest and largest mystery-specialty bookstore in America.

The shop stocks the finest selection of new mystery hardcovers, paperbacks, and periodicals. It also features a superb collection of signed modern first editions, rare and collectable works, and Sherlock Holmes titles. The bookshop issues a free monthly newsletter highlighting its book clubs, new releases, events, and recently acquired books.

58 Warren Street
info@mysteriousbookshop.com
(212) 587-1011
Monday through Saturday
11:00 a.m. to 7:00 p.m.

FIND OUT MORE AT:

www.mysteriousbookshop.com

FOLLOW US:

@TheMysterious and Facebook.com/MysteriousBookshop

INTEGRATED MEDIA

Find a full list of our authors and
titles at www.openroadmedia.com

FOLLOW US
@OpenRoadMedia